COLE FOR CHRISTMAS

KELLY COLLINS

BOOK NOOK PRESS

The trees were decorated with love and care... with all my heart.

PRAISE AND AWARDS

"What a hidden gem to find!"

~ Panty Dropping Book Blog-Kathy

"Thank you Kelly Collins for creating an awesome love story that was truly an enjoyable little escape for me."

~For the Love of Books

"When you read a book by an author you never know what to expect. It's either YAY or NAY. Kelly Collins is defiantly a YAY!"

~British Book Binge

CHAPTER 1

I had a feeling my life was going to change from the moment I woke up. It could have been wishful thinking, but the sun was brighter and the air crisper. Maybe it felt different because I was desperate for change.

I pulled in front of 35 Thunder Ridge Lane and allowed myself a moment of unbridled envy. The multistory stone and timber home stood by itself at the end of Thunder Bowl. It was the perfect ski-in and ski-out home. In the distance, snowboarders raced down the mountain at breakneck speed, kicking up clouds of powder in their wake. The bowl was for daredevils and pros not beginners like me. When the owner had called, he'd been desperate for a decorator, and I'd been desperate for a paycheck. Breaking into the Aspen scene had been impossible. Since my arrival early last summer, I'd been shunned at every turn. Tight-knit communities full of rich people didn't open their homes or wallets to strangers.

I hoped the housekeeper had left the key by the front door as promised. I had three days to transform this house into a winter wonderland, and I'd need every minute. Mr. Cole's family was arriving December twenty-third, and he wanted his house decked for Christmas. His exact words were, "I want to give Norman Rockwell a run for his money."

As promised, the key was tucked into the topiary by the front door. It slid smoothly into the lock and with a gentle turn, the door fell open. *Wow.* The great room was . . . well . . . great. So great time stilled as I took in the grandeur of a home many could appreciate but few could afford.

A stone fireplace stretched from the hardwood floors all the way to the twenty-foot beamed ceilings. The sixteen-foot tree I'd purchased today would be perfect tucked between the fireplace and the wall of glass.

It took pinching myself to be certain I wasn't dreaming. I was really in this house, doing this job, *and* earning a paycheck. Out of habit, I began to mentally note my plan of attack. It would take several hours to put the tree together before I could get to the fun stuff—decorating. If the temp agency came through, that time would be cut in half. Hired help was a luxury I couldn't afford, but efficiency was worth the price, and an extra body would be a boon.

Thankfully, Mr. Cole had given me an ample budget. I didn't blink an eye when the tree cost around three thousand dollars. A good quality tree would last many years.

I hoped this job would be my breakout project. It was also my ticket to making it through the winter. I refused to fail. To crawl back to Los Angeles and beg Ryan for help would be unbearable. I couldn't imagine bringing myself so low. I left with my clothes, my car, and my dignity, and now realize I don't need much more than that.

Note to self, *never* sleep with the boss again.

"Hello," a deep voice called from the front door.

I whipped around to see tall, dark, and muscular. "Thank the Lord. I'm so glad you're here." I tossed him the keys. "Open the trailer and start by bringing in the tree. It's in the five boxes toward the back." He hardly seemed prepared for the task. Dressed in khakis and a button-down shirt, he looked more suited for selling the house than decorating it.

I'd expected a long-haired ski bum, not a down-on-his-luck pretty boy. I hoped the man could work because I had no intention of going easy on him since he failed to dress for the job. However, those muscles would be an asset.

"I'm—" He reached to shake my hand, but I shook my head and pointed toward the door.

"We can get chummy later. Right now I need you to get the tree out of the trailer." Surprise lit his eyes. "I have three days to get this house ready. When Mr. Cole brings his family here, I want them to feel like Christmas couldn't exist anywhere else." He was standing there looking at me like I'd grown antlers. If he didn't step into gear, I'd have to send him packing. I wasn't going to pay for lackluster performance. "Move it." And he was out the door.

I suppose I should have let him introduce himself. I would remedy that as soon as he brought the first box through the door. It's not my norm to be rude, but the hours would evaporate if I dallied, and a rushed job was never a good job.

While he muscled the tree boxes from the trailer, I muscled the furniture into a new Christmas-tree-friendly arrangement. The fireplace and tree had to take center stage. However, the large A-frame window was too beautiful to ignore.

Whoever decorated this space originally did an outstanding job. The furniture was versatile and worked well when separated. The soft leather sofa was a perfect fit in front of the fireplace. With the massive tree to the right, it would be a comfortable place to camp out on Christmas morning and open presents.

I closed my eyes and visualized it complete. Flickering lights. Festive bulbs. Family. All necessary ingredients for a memorable holiday.

"Where do you want the first box?" The man had a sexy-as-all-get-out voice. The kind that made you clench your thighs and need to change your underwear.

"Bring it here. By the way, I'm Chloe Craig, but most people call me Cici. I'm sorry I was so rude earlier. You have no idea how important this job is to me. It's been hard to get a foothold in the industry here, and this job is like getting a golden ticket."

"Elias, my name is Elias." He stopped at his first name and that worked for me. The less chitchat the better.

"Well, Elias, seeing you come through the door made my day. I wasn't sure the service would send someone." Something flashed across his face. I wasn't sure what I'd seen in his eyes, but I would have sworn it was humor. "It looks like Tannenbaum Temps has done me a solid." Maybe like me, he was happy to be employed.

"Where do you want this?" He pushed the box across

the floor until I bolted forward and threw myself on top to stop him.

"No, you could scratch the floor. This is a multimillion-dollar home, and let me tell you, you may look like you could live here, but neither of us can afford to refinish these floors." I circled him to look for damage. No scratches. *Whew.* "Rich people don't take kindly to employees ruining their homes. If you're going to work with me, you're going to have to pay closer attention to our client's belongings."

"Duly noted." He groaned while he hefted the box off the floor and carried it to the window.

"Those shoes are going to kill your feet by the end of the day." He stared down at his leather loafers and shrugged. "If you hope to work with me again, I suggest you work hard today and think about dressing more appropriately tomorrow." I wasn't sure he was going to work out, but I'd be darned if I sent him home before the heavy lifting was done. Besides, he was easy on the eyes.

I pulled a scrunchie from my pocket and twisted my hair into a high ponytail. Not the most flattering look, but one that made sense for a full day's work. I didn't have the time or patience to deal with my out-of-control hair. I suppose I should be grateful I'd inherited the Craig curls. I was low maintenance: just wash, toss, and go.

While Elias left to get the next box, I thought through my plan of attack and began.

The base of the tree fit perfectly into the space I'd chosen. I began to insert the color-coded branches into their corresponding colored slots. Elias continued to carry in boxes. I was on number two when he had carried in box five. His poor shirt was drenched in sweat. Beads of perspiration rolled down his face and dripped from his dark curls onto his collar. I was tempted to reach up and wipe his brow. The poor man looked miserable. He was obviously not used to manual labor, and I wondered why Tannenbaum sent him. I was sure I'd put heavy lifting in the job description. I couldn't fault his work though; he was quick and didn't complain.

"On the front seat of my SUV is a cooler with a variety of drinks from water to soda. Help yourself." I turned around and went back to placing branches into their slots. He walked toward the door, and I called to him, "After you get a drink, bring in the ladder. We'll need it to assemble the rest of the tree."

He lugged in the ladder and set it up next to the tree. I loved that I didn't have to tell him what to do. I'd worked with some clueless people, and often it took more time to explain than to do the job myself. Today was looking up. It was a bit rocky at first. Just goes to show you, you shouldn't judge a person by their Italian loafers.

"What does a tree this size cost?" He pulled a branch from the box and looked for its color-coordinated slot.

"These run anywhere from twenty-five hundred up to the tens of thousands. I was able to get this one for just under three grand with it being so late in the season. I used my designer's discount and got an extra ten percent off." I tugged the next section out of the box and climbed the ladder to slide it into the existing pole. The tree was well over seven feet at this point but we still had nine feet to go.

"So will you charge your client the original amount and pocket the rest? That would seem the prudent thing to do." He stood by the ladder and steadied it as if he were afraid I'd fall. Hell, I'd spent half my life on ladders.

"No way. I always pass on the discount to my client. The ten percent is nothing, but a follow-up job is everything. Hand me the red-coded branches."

He began to hand them to me one by one. Thankfully, his sweaty face had dried, and the red had left his neck. The last thing I needed was pretty boy to get overheated and need medical attention.

"What do you do for a living, Elias? You're doing a fine job, but this obviously isn't in your lane." I pulled the branch from his hand and giggled at his look of surprise.

"I'm not sure if I should be pleased or offended."

"Don't be offended. Look at your hands. There isn't a callous anywhere, and you have fingernails prettier than mine. I should be offended." I shoved another branch into the center pole. We were making quick work of the tree.

"I can't lie to you. I'm more an office worker than a manual labor kind of guy, but I'm not afraid of getting my hands dirty."

"I got that impression." I brushed the sweat off my forehead and wiped my hand on my jeans. I always dressed clean but casual for my job. Today was no different. The polo shirt I wore had Craig Designs above the left breast. It felt good to represent myself rather than Ryan Westland Design Company.

For the next hour, we worked side by side, assembling branch after branch. I placed the perfectly pointed pine branch on top. The way it filled the space was perfect. Mr. Cole had a good eye for measurements, as it was the exact height needed for the room. He'd said the ceilings were about twenty feet high, and he was spot on.

"What do you think?" I stood back and admired our work. It looked great now, but once it was decorated, it would be breathtaking.

"It's all right." He shrugged his shoulders and walked to the wall of windows. He was obviously not a man who appreciated the holidays.

"This is going to come out great. I'm glad the owner isn't present. I hate it when they're around. It slows down the process. Normally, I wouldn't take on a house sight unseen, but the poor man sounded desperate, and I was equally desperate for a job."

He'd said he was out of town and his girlfriend had dropped the ball. The phone connection had been bad, but we'd managed to get the details covered before we were disconnected. Since that first call, we'd communicated through texting.

"Why so desperate?" He turned to look my way. Too bad the guy was broke. He would have made good dating material. Shame I couldn't afford to take care of both of us.

"I had a falling out with my last company and moved to Aspen for a fresh start. This is my first job."

"Welcome to Aspen. Do you ski?" His question caught me by surprise. I suppose it shouldn't have since he was looking longingly out the window at the ski run. People like us couldn't afford to ski. We watched while others raced down the slopes.

"I don't think what I do can be called skiing. I imagine I'm more of a snowplower than an actual skier. You?" I began to fold down the boxes to get them out of the way. It was time for the fun to begin.

"Love it. The lessons I took a few years back really

helped my form. You should think about hiring an instructor."

I had no idea what he thought I made, but an instructor was out of the question this year. Every dime I earned needed to get me through the winter. I had rent to pay and food to buy, not to mention car payments to be made.

"I'll have to look into that. Can you start bringing in the other boxes? They're full of lights and decorations. I figure if we can get the tree done today, we can work on wreaths and garlands tomorrow. I want to use live materials so the pine smell infuses the air. There's nothing like the smell of pine in winter. I'm also going to use lots of cinnamon sticks so the house smells like freshly baked goods."

"You've got this whole thing down, don't you?" He piled the flattened boxes into his arms and carried them out the front door. Moments later he returned with two full boxes and a bottle of cold water in his back pocket. "Here, you need to stay hydrated. The altitude can really take a lot out of you. Drink up."

I was touched by his consideration and gladly took the water, gulping down half of it. I was so intent on getting the tree up, I hadn't considered thirst or dehydration.

We took a short break to eat lunch. I happily shared the couple of peanut butter and jelly sandwiches I'd brought with me. He'd come unprepared.

The rest of the job was like opening boxes on Christmas morning. I loved the holidays, and decorating the Christmas tree was always my favorite activity. I usually had a six-footer. Imagine the fun I was going to have with sixteen feet.

Elias looked less than enthused. "Don't you enjoy decorating a tree?" I plugged in the lights and watched them twinkle to life. This tree's stationary and blinking lights would keep it in perpetual illumination.

"I just don't see the point. You spend a ton of time putting something up that you'll just tear down and destroy in a week or so. It seems like a waste of time and resources, but it's important to some people. I get that, so I go with the flow."

"Well, get with the flow and start placing the decorative picks in between the branches. We have garland and ribbon to hang before we get to the bulbs. I think we have a thousand of them to place before we get to the candy canes. Mr. Cole didn't tell me whether there were children or not, but young or old, a tree isn't a tree without peppermint treats."

"I like peppermint." He moved to the opposite side of the tree and began to place the picks.

We spent the next couple hours working from the top of the tree to the bottom. Elias was slow to catch on, but once he did, he seemed to get into the spirit. I played Christmas music on my iPhone, and we hung the tree jewelry to songs like "Deck the Halls" and "Grandma Got Run Over by a Reindeer."

I explained the symbolism of the Christmas tree, and he sounded surprised when I told him the evergreen symbolized undying life. Christmas was about hope and love. Add in everything else like stars and balls, bows and candy canes, and you had an extravaganza of delight.

"Do we have a star?" Did I hear a hint of excitement in his voice?

"Of course we have a star." I pulled out an ornate

topper made from pearlized glass. Lit from the inside, it would throw off prisms of light that would shine across the wooden ceiling. The star was a foot tall and would take the height of our masterpiece to seventeen feet.

I offered the star to Elias. He gave me a strange look and shook his head. I pushed the star into his hand and told him to get his ass up the ladder and place the crowning glory on the tree. From his horrified expression, you would have thought I'd handed him a scalpel and told him to perform a triple bypass.

He climbed the ladder slowly. "I don't like heights." His knees wobbled, and his face paled.

I climbed behind him and held onto his shaking calves. Man, he had muscular legs. "You'll go on a ski lift, but you won't climb a ladder?" I wanted to run my hands all the way up his thighs and squeeze the cheeks I knew would be firm under my grasp, but I didn't dare. He was a day hire, and I was his boss.

"I don't look down, and there's a payoff when skiing. Nothing good comes with ladders." He reached up and slid the star over the center. "Why are you so comfortable with heights?" He fumbled with the cord, and I felt his whole body shake while he reached farther to push the plug into the waiting socket attached to the tree.

"My dad's a painter, and I spent my childhood helping him. I grew up on a ladder." Just then, the star lit up, and light shot out from each point, spilling across the room. Breathtaking. Given the bright smile on his face, even Elias seemed to be feeling happy.

We'd put in a good day's work, and I invited Elias to come back tomorrow. He was a hard worker and was open to suggestion. That went a long way with me, but when I asked him to come back he busted into thunderous laughter and told me he would be here. No wonder he was unemployed, he was weird.

He folded the ladder and walked it to my trailer. When he returned, I was sitting on the sofa in a room lit only by the Christmas tree. Stunning. I'd never seen one as beautiful. I knew I could do a good job, but I had no idea how amazing seventeen feet of glass balls, satin ribbon, and peppermint candy could look. I only hoped Christmas joy might reach Elias too. Shame I couldn't help with that.

CHAPTER 2

Snow had been coming down all night long. Inches of the fluffy white stuff covered everything in sight. I inched my SUV up the driveway and parked in front of the same garage door as yesterday. I was a creature of habit, and that parking place had temporarily become mine.

Would Elias be waiting by the door? I glanced around but didn't see him. A feeling of disappointment sank heavily in my stomach. I liked him. He didn't talk much about himself, but he wasn't bad company. Today would go much slower with his absence, and the view wouldn't be as pleasant.

Golden lights backlit the windows. I was certain I'd turned off everything before I left yesterday. In fact, I went in twice to make sure. I never wanted to be thought of as irresponsible when it came to other people's property.

Maybe Mr. Cole had arrived. My heart skipped a beat

at the thought. In an ideal situation the owners would be absent until the big reveal, then they would show up and ooh and ahh over the transformation. I'd collect my check and be on my way.

I killed the engine and climbed out of the warm cab into the cold air. My jacket was zipped all the way to my neck, the collar pulled around my ears. I trudged through the snow to my trailer. Dozens of fresh garlands and several wreaths were sitting in the back, waiting to make their holiday debut. With some strategically placed pine cones and ribbons, I would transform a strip of plain pine into a thing of beauty. Today, the focus would be on the mantel and stairs, tomorrow the entry and kitchen. *Watch out, Norman Rockwell.*

I gave another look-see, hoping Elias would appear out of thin air, but he was nowhere to be found. Maybe I'd scared him away. "Dance of the Sugar Plum Fairy" began to play on my phone. I themed my ringtones to the season.

"Hello." I recognized the nasally tone right away. The owner of Tannenbaum Temps could have given Fran Drescher a run for her money. In a blind auditory test, it would have been tough to tell them apart.

"Hi, Chloe. I just wanted to call and apologize for not being able to send anyone over yesterday." *Did she just say she was sorry no one showed yesterday? Surely she was mistaken.* "Everyone seems to be needing extra help, and there wasn't anyone to spare." The rrrrr dragged on for a lifetime.

"Elias came." I wanted to tell her she could rent him as eye candy, but that seemed unprofessional, and I was still trying to slide my foot through the tiny crack in the door to Aspen. "He did a great job. Thanks."

"I'm so glad you found someone else. I hope you'll use us again." The woman had lost her sugar cookies. I'd found Elias through her. Not wanting to push the point, I thanked her and hung up. With Elias a no-show, I was on my own today. I pulled a box of evergreens from the trailer and plowed my way to the front door.

Given the lights on inside, I rang the bell. Better safe than sorry. A shadow darkened the window. The bubbled glass distorted the figure making it impossible to see who was behind the door. I shifted the heavy box in my hands and waited.

Elias stood in front of me barefoot, dressed in blue jeans and a snug-fitting gray T-shirt. Bright lights from the tree danced across the walls and ceiling, and the sizzle and pop of burning logs from the fireplace reached out to me, beckoning me toward its cozy warmth. *What the hell? He* looked perfect standing where he didn't belong, but what on earth did he think he was doing?

"What the hell are you doing in the house?" The box in my hands dropped to the floor along with my jaw. "You can't enter the house without me. That's unprofessional. I'm going to have to report you to your boss."

"Cici, let me explain." He rocked between his bare feet.

"You're fired." I slipped my boots off because melted snow and hardwood floors didn't mix well. "You can't go into people's houses and make yourself comfortable." Picking up the box of evergreens, I pushed my way past him and walked toward the fireplace where I placed the box on the floor. When I glanced around the room everything appeared to be in order.

Thank God he hadn't emptied the house in my absence.

"Cici," he said, almost pleading. I had to give him credit for being persistent and brave.

"No, you have to go." Burning rage coiled within me. "I don't want to hear your excuses. You took advantage of our client. You took advantage of me. Now you're unemployed. Hit the road." This was my first chance to make a name for myself, and I wasn't going to let a temp ruin my reputation. "Out." My pitch hit high altitude. If he didn't start moving soon, I was going to drag him by the ear and toss him out the door, bare feet notwithstanding.

When he began to laugh, I began to shake. What did I get myself into hiring this man? He was missing a cog in his brain.

"Cici. We have to clear the air." He made his way into the great room and sank into the leather sofa like he owned it.

"Don't get comfortable." The tone of my voice had fallen to a normal level. I was obviously speaking with a deranged man and the appearance of calm was necessary. "If I have to, I'll call the police." I spoke in a slow and steady stream, which was in direct conflict with my pounding heart. *Doom da da doom da da doom* beat against my rib cage like a percussionist banging the bass drum.

"Cici, I'm Elias Cole. I own the house." The words raced from his mouth like a downhill skier trying to qualify for a run.

Doom da da doom da da doom rose from my chest and beat in my head until I was dizzy from the sound.

"Wait . . . What?" Holy shit. I pushed that man like a

slave master yesterday. I said things to him I would've never said to a client. "You lied to me." I choked out the words and tried to swallow the excess saliva that threatened to choke me.

"I did no such thing." His voice played at full volume. "You decided on your own who I was, and I opted not to correct you."

If I weren't so shocked I'd have been angry.

"Why would you do that? You stayed under false pretenses and allowed me to believe you were someone you weren't." My perfect job was disintegrating before my eyes. "In my book that's lying."

"It wasn't my intention to lead you astray. You looked like you needed help."

"I thought you were the help. If I had known—"

"You would have behaved differently. I liked that you were open and honest. Would you have been that way if you knew who I was?"

He had a point. I would have told him to do what I was going to tell him now.

"You have to leave. You can't be here while I work." I snapped the lid of the box open and began spreading the pine garland on the floor.

"That's bullshit. I was here all day yesterday while you worked, and it turned out fine. I'm staying." He crossed his arms over his chest and sank deeper into the cognac-colored cushions.

Even angry with him, I couldn't deny how cute he was. Damn man.

"You're a distraction, and I have a job to do." He'd been a distraction yesterday. Today he'd be a complete roadblock. He and his perfectly shaped bare feet needed to move along.

He kicked his feet up on the coffee table. It had to be his way of telling me he wasn't budging. I would have pushed the issue, but the snow was falling hard, and I didn't have the heart to send him into the cold. If only he wasn't tall, dark, and gorgeous. That would make ignoring a whole lot easier.

Boots on. Boots off. I made several trips between the house and trailer. All the while Elias watched my every move.

"I could help you today." His voice sounded hopeful.

"I've got it." I pulled at the red ribbon, trying to get it to behave. "You're paying me to decorate your house, and I intend to do it by myself." Once I beat the bow into submission, I tacked it onto the garland. "My company is called Craig Design, not Craig and Cole Design. Thanks for the offer though."

Shit, I owed him a paycheck. I would have paid the temp fifteen dollars an hour. I'd bring him a check tomorrow.

He sat on the couch and watched while I wove pine bows into thick plush ropes and decorated them with red ribbons, pine cones, and Christmas bulbs. I layered row upon row on the mantel. The bulbs and bows I tied to the greenery brought life to the arrangement. The heat from the fireplace released the scent of the cinnamon sticks I had tucked throughout.

Most of the time Elias appeared to be lost in thought while he stared at the fireplace. After an hour or so, he shifted and stood. Thank God he was finally leaving. He only made it a few steps before turning back.

"I'm making cheese omelets. Care to join me?" He spun and walked toward what had to be the kitchen. "I think I owe you," he said over his shoulder.

"I'd love an omelet. Just eggs and cheese, right?" I couldn't be mad at a man who wanted to feed me, and I liked eggs and cheese. Besides, I had to get a good look at the kitchen so I could pretty it up tomorrow.

I followed him into a kitchen. *Wow*. A kitchen designed for a chef; this one had double ovens, a Wolf gas range, and a Sub-Zero refrigerator. Sleek granite countertops and marble floors. Simply wow.

"Yep, just eggs and cheese. Eggs are about the only thing I can cook." He slid out a stool from the island and patted the granite counter in front of it. My cue to sit.

"What do you do for a living, Mr. Cole?" He moved comfortably around the kitchen. It was hard getting used to the idea that he owned the place. No wonder he seemed at home yesterday.

"Call me Elias." He pulled a bottle of orange juice from the refrigerator and poured two glasses. It was well after noon, and here we were eating breakfast. "We don't have to move backward just because our roles have changed."

"Well, Elias, what's your line of work?" He didn't seem old enough to own this house. I'd guess he was in his mid-thirties. Maybe he came from money.

"Real estate. I buy and sell property. I've done pretty well." He stood tall when he spoke. He was obviously proud of his accomplishments and who wouldn't be? This house was a gold mine.

"You live here in Aspen?" I sipped my orange juice. It was the high-pulp variety I loved.

"Not full time." He broke the eggs one at a time and let

them fall into a bowl he had set on the counter. "I have a house in the Cherry Creek area of Denver, but I've been thinking of moving here permanently." With steady turns of his wrist, he whipped the eggs with precision. "I'm not sure there's enough property to keep me busy. Besides, the competition is tough."

"I understand about competition. I've been here since early summer. Originally, I wanted to work at an existing firm, but no one would give me a chance, so I created my own opportunity by opening Craig Design."

"This is a tough community. I was an outsider for many years, but that all changed when I joined the country club." The mixture sizzled when poured it into the heated pan.

"Don't tell me that. I could never afford the country club." I couldn't afford to spring for a fitness club. A country club was way out of my reach. "How does someone like me get her foot in the door?"

"Word of mouth. You're doing an excellent job. I'll pass the word around." He put three kinds of cheese into the center of the omelet.

I loved cheese, and three was like hitting a trifecta.

"Thanks. Maybe I'll get some additional Christmas work next year, but I have to figure out something before then." I rose from the table and walked to where he stood.

"Have you considered staging homes? It's a huge thing here." He poked at the air bubbles that had risen on the eggs before he flipped the pan and the mixture folded in half into the perfect omelet. "Above your head are the plates, can you grab two?"

White plates were stacked ten high in front of me.

Square plates. Not mainstream, but I liked them. It said he was a risk-taker not a conformist.

"No, I've never staged a house for sale, but I've decorated plenty of homes for clients. It couldn't be that tough." Did I have what it takes to do that?

He slid the omelet onto the plate and handed it to me along with a mountain-themed fork. The handle was shaped like a branch. Too cute.

"Don't underestimate the skill it takes. You have to make a home look neutral but appeal to a wide range of buyers. That's not easy." While we were talking, he had poured the remaining eggs into the pan and whipped together a second omelet. "There's good money to be made in Aspen if you can breach the market. If you're interested, I'll introduce you around. Hell, I have a house listing in January that will need staging. Let me know." He slid his omelet onto a plate and sat by my side while we devoured our delicious brunch.

"I appreciate the advice." I'd become whatever I had to become in order to make ends meet. "I'll look into it and let you know." Real estate sales weren't necessarily in my lane, but I'd drive there if it meant food on the table and a roof over my head. I had to make this work. There was no going back.

"What brought you to Colorado?"

My normal answer would have been I needed a change of pace, which wasn't entirely untrue. I did need a change of pace, but what I needed most was distance. "I wanted to leave Los Angeles. New York was too far away so I picked a place in between." That was the truth or at least most of the truth. "When I decided to relocate, I looked at the map and picked someplace in the middle of the country. That someplace was Nebraska, but I couldn't bring myself to live in a state that was flat and had an entire population smaller than the city I had lived in."

"Why leave Los Angeles? Wasn't it the perfect place to be an interior designer?" He drew a bite of omelet to his lips, a melted wisp of cheese hung from the corner of his mouth. His tongue dipped out to grab it, and my heart began to race.

"The normal reasons: bad breakup and a job loss. Both on the same day." That summed it up. Quickly. Honestly

"Sorry. I shouldn't have pressed." While he stared forward sipping his juice, I stared at him. He was one of those men who would remain forever young—evergreen. His eyes were Caribbean blue with specks of brown near the center. The exact color of the granite I had installed in the last California home I decorated.

Sitting here and staring at him, although pleasant, seemed wrong. He wasn't available, and I wasn't interested. But I was curious, and he was too sexy for me to completely ignore.

"Tell me about your girlfriend." Well, shit, my mouth opened before my brain could stop me.

"Not much to tell. We've been dating for a couple months. She's busy in her job, I'm busy in mine, and we seem to meet in the middle."

He gave no details about his girlfriend, which made me curious about the kind of woman he'd pick. "Well, I hope she likes the decorations." I lifted up our empty plates and walked them to the sink.

Elias remained in the kitchen while I went to work on the banisters. About an hour into my work, I heard yelling. I hoped I was never on the receiving end of that tone. That anger.

"What the hell do you mean you're not coming for Christmas?" His pitch rose until I was certain the volume could have started an avalanche.

Silence.

"That's bullshit, and you know it. I took the whole week off to be with you and my parents."

Silence.

I shouldn't have stood there and listened, but I couldn't move. There was something in his voice that kept me glued in place. He was angry, but he sounded hurt, and I was a sucker for hurt.

"So you're spending the holiday with him? How long has it been going on? I see. No. I don't share. I need to be with someone who values me and what I have to offer."

Silence.

"No, you're not that person. What? It was never about sex. Hell, I could count the times we've had sex on one hand."

He turned around and saw me staring. Pain was etched into his face. In less than an hour, he seemed to have aged several years. "Sorry." It was all I could say after I'd been caught eavesdropping. I spun around and took off toward the stairs.

I worked for hours and only saw Elias once after the fight. He entered what I assumed was his office but never came out. I felt sorry for the man. I knew what it was like to be dumped. That conversation was reminiscent of the one I'd had with Ryan. My heart ached for Elias. Breakups were hard, but when the other person was unfaithful, the breakup seemed nearly unbearable. Was the girl stupid?

Elias was perfection. Well, from the short time I've known him anyway. He's funny, generous, kind, and obviously a hard worker. He didn't flinch when I told him what to do yesterday. And, let's not forget, easy on the eyes.

I looped fresh garland between the rungs of the banister and tied bows and pine cones to liven up the look. I finished the day with the wreaths I'd hung above the fireplace mantel and the front door. Uncomfortable leaving without saying goodbye, I tapped lightly on the office door.

"Come in." He sat in a black leather chair behind a rosewood desk. Papers were placed in neat piles across the top. Everything appeared in order except his life. The light in his eyes had dimmed, giving him a look of a tired and worn-out man.

"I just wanted to tell you I'm leaving for the day. I'll be back to finish tomorrow. If you have a chance to look over my work I'd appreciate it. I want to make sure you're satisfied with what I've done thus far."

"Cici, so far everything has been great. My family will love it." He pushed back from the chair and rose from his seat. His feet were still bare. That was a benefit of under-floor heating. At my place, I'd have had ten toesicles.

"But I want you to fall in love." His eyes widened at my remark. It was the right sentiment, but the wrong words given he'd just had a falling out with who I believed to be his girlfriend.

It was reassuring to know his family would love it, but I was more concerned with him than anyone else. I would have liked to say it was because he was the client, but truthfully, I liked him. Given his present circumstances, I wanted something to bring joy to his life. Too bad he was such a tough sell when it came to the holidays.

"It's fine." He led me to the front door and all but pushed me forward. When it closed behind me, I was hell-bent on making sure by the time I finished tomorrow, things would go from it's fine to it's fabulous.

CHAPTER 3

Being late was not in my plan, but given the circumstances at the Cole house, I wanted to give Elias a little extra. I'd purchased the planned items then picked up some fun holiday treats I hoped he would enjoy, and those extra stops put me behind schedule. In the backseat was a gift. I couldn't leave him a sixteen-foot tree without a gift beneath it. It was a silly gift only he would understand, and the beautiful wrap job was worth more than the contents.

When he came to the door, he was dressed in a suit and tie and looked commanding. Gone was the vulnerability of yesterday. This man had dressed to impress. To conquer the day.

"Wow. Look at you. All dressed up and someplace to go." I walked past him and headed straight for the kitchen. He trailed behind me.

"I'm closing on a house today. Kind of a Christmas bonus." He picked up his juice glass from the counter and

"

rinsed it out. I loved a man who could take care of himself.

"Speaking of Christmas bonuses . . . Even though you were working under false pretenses," I looked at him with a *don't-argue-with-me* look—the one that kept most people's mouths shut—"I brought you a check for your hours. I'm sure it's a pittance compared to what you normally make, but I'm an honest businesswoman, and I wouldn't feel right about you working without pay." I put the folded check into his front breast pocket and gave it a pat.

"I'm not taking your money. Working with you was fun." He tried to remove the check, but I gave him my look and added a snarl. He laughed and stepped back.

"Will I see you before I finish today?" I hoped he would say yes, but I could see in his eyes it was doubtful. It didn't matter. I'd leave my little treats and hope he finds some joy in them.

"Probably not, but you never know. Thanks so much, Cici. Just send me the bill, and I'll pay it immediately. My family arrives the day after tomorrow so this worked out perfectly." He stood awkwardly before me. At first, he opened his arms like he would hug me, and then he leaned in like he was going to give me a peck on the cheek. In the end, he offered me a disappointing handshake.

I grabbed his hand and pulled him into my arms. It wasn't a passionate hug. Just the type of hug you gave a friend when they needed one. When he stood back, his neck had turned red and his cheeks pink. So, Mr. Cole was shy. I wouldn't have thought that given his success.

He started for the door but turned back toward me

like he was going to say something. He paused for a long breath, shook his head, and turned toward the door again. His suit looked as impressive from the backside as it did from the front. There was something about a navy blue pinstripe suit that did it for me.

The throaty growl of his car had me running to the front door to watch him pull away. I'd have never taken him for a Range Rover type, but the black SUV looked sexy wrapped around him.

See you later, Mr. Tall, Dark, and Delicious. Thanks for my Christmas treat.

Today was all about accessorizing and sprucing up what I'd done before. I filled three glass apothecary jars with edibles. One was stuffed with mini candy canes, one with chocolate Santas, and the third with Christmas gummy trees. The jars were decorative yet functional. Maybe Elias would see *the point* of these.

I set other little treats around the house. A bowl of pretty wrapped truffles decorated the end table by the window. A red candle embossed with gold filigree and pine needles was centered on the coffee table. When it came to the porch, two four-foot pine topiaries flanked the front door. With their twinkling lights, it would be warm and inviting at night.

Just above the front door, I hung mistletoe. What was Christmas without mistletoe and kisses? It was depressing to think this would be my first year in a while without a kiss or hug.

It was just about time for me to leave, and I'd almost forgotten his gift. I raced to my SUV and pulled the box from the backseat. Looking at the decorations with fresh eyes when I entered the house, it could have been right out of a magazine. I felt proud. The only thing missing was a mountain of presents under the tree. I slipped my silly gift beneath the pine boughs and walked to the kitchen.

He needed to get into the spirit of things, especially if his family was coming soon, so my challenge sat front and center for Elias. There were four days until Christmas, and he needed to get in touch with his inner Kris Kringle. I had purchased a gingerbread man kit and had hoped to persuade him to give it a try. I hoped he saw the fun in my note and wasn't offended.

Dear Mr. Scrooge,

It's time you embraced the season. It's almost Christmas, and I'm here to remind you to find the love and joy this holiday has to offer. Enjoy your family and enjoy your decorated home. Thanks for allowing me the opportunity to work for you. Please don't hesitate to call should you need additional assistance. This poor gingerbread man needs some clothes. Do your best!

Cici

Tonight I would celebrate. I walked out of his house feeling accomplished. Whole Foods was calling me. Eggplant parmigiana for dinner and ambrosia cake for dessert would be my treat for a job well done.

I sat in front of the TV with my microwaved eggplant and watched the old classic *Miracle on 34th Street.* I believed in miracles. I didn't think there was an old guy named Kris Kringle waiting to buy me a house, but I believed the holidays were magical.

Sadly, I didn't have the money to travel home to California, and my parents didn't fly. My dad said *if God wanted him to fly He would have given me wings.* I used to come back at him with *if God wanted you to drive He would have given you tires.* It never worked.

Nope, this holiday would be spent with my goldfish, Jax, and my remote control. In the corner of my living room stood my Charlie Brown tree.

I'd found the saddest looking tree on the lot and brought it home. The guy running the tree farm tried to give it to me for free, but I handed him a ten and told him everything had value. It didn't have the elaborate decorations of Elias's tree, but I was able to turn a few sad twigs into a proud symbol of the season.

Snuggled into the cushions of my couch and tucked up under the afghan my mother had crocheted for me last Christmas, I watched the television intently as thousands of letters were dumped on the judge's desk. I'd seen this movie no less than thirty times, and I was still captivated.

"Dance of the Sugar Plum Fairy" rang in the background. I raced to the kitchen, trying to reach my phone before the fairy was silenced.

"Hello." Breathless, I sucked in air until my lungs were full. When would I get used to the high altitude and thin air?

"Hey, Cici, it's Elias." His voice was like aged cognac on a cold day. It warmed you from the inside out.

A thousand things ran through my head in an instant. Was he happy? Was he disappointed? Did he decorate his gingerbread man?

"Hi, what's up?" I attempted to sound nonchalant. Unfazed.

"I read your note, and I'm taking you up on your offer. I'm at a disadvantage. I need help Christmas shopping. Becca and I were supposed to go together tomorrow." Dead silence filled the space. Cue the crickets. "Well, you know what happened there. Can I hire you to go shopping for me? I've never been good at picking out women's gifts, and I'd like to get my mom something better than a gift card and a candle. When it comes to my sis, I'm at a complete loss."

There was desperation in his voice. He had his house decorated for his family, and he wanted their holiday to be perfect. That would require heartfelt gifts. Of course, I would help him, but I wouldn't do it for him. I didn't know his mother or his sister and wasn't qualified to go that course alone. There were some things women loved universally, like jewelry, but he would need to come along in order to get the perfect gift.

"Absolutely. I'm happy to help, but you have to come along and give me insight into who your family is and what they like."

There was a lengthy pause. "Okay, that makes sense."

"When do you want me to be at your house?" We would need to start early. The stores would be crowded and the traffic horrendous. Last-minute shoppers always drove me crazy.

"I'll pick you up at nine." I could hear the relief in his voice. "We can grab breakfast out. My treat." He almost sounded excited. I gave him my address and told him I'd be ready when he arrived.

When Elias pulled up, I was waiting outside. The snow sparkled like diamonds under the morning sun. Dressed in black slacks and a royal blue blouse, I stepped gingerly across the icy walkway, not wanting to ass-plant myself with a wrong step. The last thing I needed was an injury and a cold ass.

By the time I got to his SUV, he was standing next to it with the door open. Manners weren't something every man possessed. Many men thought an independent woman wanted to do everything herself. I still wanted to feel like a woman when I was with a man, so I appreciated the gesture. Feeling cared for, respected, and valued were three important things to me.

"Thank you." I slid into the heated passenger seat and buckled up while he rounded the vehicle. How sweet that he warmed my seat.

"First breakfast, then shopping. I've heard you shouldn't shop on an empty stomach." He put the car in gear and we were off.

"I think that saying is for food shopping, but it's a good idea to be well fed. I'd hate for your inner Scrooge to take over while we shop for your family." I reached over and tapped him on the arm. Today he was dressed casually. Khakis and a polo shirt. "How did the closing go?"

He looked surprised as if it was odd for someone to ask. Was it rude to ask?

"Smooth. I'm a stickler for efficiency, so I always get there early to make sure everything is in order." He pulled into the parking lot of this little dive called Sage. "Thanks for asking." *Was that a hint of a smile I saw?* Mr. Grumpy could be swayed toward the light side. Nice to know.

"Efficiency is important. Time is money, or in my case, saving time gives me more time. I hope to turn that time into money." We stepped out of the car and walked into a restaurant that could only be considered a hole in the wall. Definitely a mom and pop shop that catered to a wide range of appetites.

We walked into the quaint café. Its checkerboard floor was worn from years of foot traffic, and pictures of colorful roosters decorated every wall. It felt homey and warm, like my grandma's kitchen. The hostess greeted us with a wide smile.

"Elias and Cici, it's good to see you. I didn't know you two were friends." Elias and I looked at each other with surprise. Mary pulled two menus from the slot next to the register and walked us to the faded booth in front of the window.

"Hey, Mary. Elias and I have been working together." I took the offered menus from her hand and gave one to Elias.

"Do you both want your usual drink?" We nodded in unison.

"It's a small world," he said, his voice filled with humor. "We have probably dined here together and never noticed."

I would have liked to argue with him over that assumption. I'd have noticed him for sure. Tall, dark, and dashing was hard to overlook.

Mary approached with a soft smile gracing her face. Two teapots of water and two packets of Earl Grey were placed on the table in the center before she left. Elias and I sat still staring at the tea. What were the odds?

"Sugar or honey?" I waited for his answer before I reached for the honey.

"Honey." He grabbed the honeypot from the window ledge and swirled the dipper around. Holding it above his cup he let the honey drip in beautiful amber ribbons into his cup. "Can I?" He reloaded the dipper and readied himself to serve me.

"Of course." His long fingers rotated the stick over my cup and delivered the perfect amount of sweetness. *Who was this man?*

Mary approached and asked for our order. I tended to order the same thing every time. Cheese omelet with artichoke hearts and mushrooms. Elias ordered an omelet called The Works. I assumed it had everything a cook could put into an omelet.

"So how long can I keep you?" He sipped his hot tea with care.

I wanted to shout forever, but that would have been too weird. Besides, I wasn't sure he would get the joke. The real problem was, I wasn't positive I'd be joking.

I glanced outside. "I'm free the whole day." The shops were opening. People were milling about. Things were springing to life. "Where are we shopping?"

"I thought we could start here, but if we can't find what we need we could trek to Denver."

"That's a far drive for Christmas presents." Being stuck in the car would have been awful. Being stuck for hours with Elias . . . not so bad.

"Now who's sounding like Scrooge?"

"Just trying to be efficient."

"I love that you tried."

"I do what I can." I loved the flash repartee. It was light and airy, a side I hadn't seen of him, but one I liked.

"First we have to settle the work thing. This is a job, therefore you have to get paid. Would five hundred be fair?" He played with his silverware, reorganizing it from left to right and back again.

"I'm not charging you to shop. I didn't have anything going on anyway, and I love the holidays. This will be fun for me." Seeing Mary approach with our meals, I promptly placed my napkin in my lap.

"Nope, I got paid when I worked with you. I'm paying you." He pulled his napkin off the table and put it in his lap just as Mary delivered his omelet. It looked like an egg-coated football. I was going to enjoy watching him eat that monstrosity.

"Oh, please. I thought I was hiring a temp. I paid you a pittance compared to what you're offering to pay me."

"I was hired for my brawn, I'm hiring you for your brain. Infinitely more valuable." He cut into his omelet, and I swear an entire farm was hiding in there. I could see ham and sausage, and every type of veggie known to man. "No negotiations."

With that said, I nodded and cut into my breakfast. It was perfect, like always. "So, tell me about your mom."

"She's like all moms. She's sweet and attentive and naggy and nosy." He smiled at me like he had divulged a plethora of usable information. I got nothing of value out of his description. At least nothing that would give me gift ideas.

"You gave me zilch. Give me examples. Is she like June Cleaver from *Leave It to Beaver* or is she Evelyn Harper from *Two and a Half Men?*" His face contorted. His lips pulled to the side, and his eyes turned skyward as if the answer would come from above. I could almost see him trying the characters on his mother like a piece of clothing.

"Do I only get those two choices?" He looked scared. I wasn't asking him to pick between heaven and hell. I needed a hint.

"No, but give me something. If you have an example, I'd love that."

He ate his food slowly and sipped his tea. I knew the minute he came up with something because he looked like a lotto player whose sixth number had been called.

"She's a mix between Clair Huxtable from *The Cosby Show* and Claire Dunphy from *Modern Family*. She has the sass and sex appeal of the first and the no-nonsense attitude of the second." He sat back in the booth looking relieved like he'd cut the red wire from an active bomb.

"Okay, I'm getting a feel for her. How old is she?" My guess would have been somewhere between fifty-five and sixty-five.

"She's fifty-two."

"How old are you?" I knew it came out sounding wrong, accusatory even, but if his mom was fifty-two, then he had to be younger than I initially thought.

"I'm thirty-two. My mom swears it wasn't a shotgun wedding, and since my parents have been married for close to thirty-three years, I suppose I have to believe her."

To my astonishment, while we were chatting, he gorged down half of his meal. I couldn't, in all honesty, call it an omelet. Omelets conjured visions of fluffy eggs filled lightly with ingredients that tickled your palate.

What he was eating was an assault on his mouth and stomach.

"That's impressive. Thirty-two, a house in Aspen, and one in a posh Denver suburb. How did you do that?" I waited for him to say trust fund or something crazier like lotto win.

"Sacrifice and hard work," he said matter-of-factly. Like all hard work leads to Aspen houses and untold riches. I'd worked my ass off, and all I had was an apartment and a savings account with next month's rent.

I didn't know him well enough to judge him, but it was obvious he wasn't afraid of hard work. I respected that in a man. "Tell me about the first house you sold." I pushed my empty plate to the side and leaned in toward him.

"It was my parents' house. I was twenty-two. I'd gotten my real estate license as a fallback to my degree in marketing." He poured more tea and twirled more honey. "I enjoyed the thrill of the sale, so I stuck with real estate."

"Seems to be a good match for you."

"It is, but I've missed a lot of Christmases and other holidays, which is why this one is so important. My family is excited to visit. I'm not sure if they are more excited to see me, the house, or my girlfriend."

"You'll have to tell them she won't be here." I lowered my head, still feeling ashamed I'd witnessed his dark moment. "By the way, I'm sorry what she did to you." I didn't want to see the pain I knew would be in his eyes, so I kept my head down.

"I'll break it to them tomorrow when they arrive." The squeak of the plate sliding against the table forced me to look up. I'd be darned. He polished off the entire thing.

"Did they know her?" That's the thing with relationships, families become attached and breakups hurt everyone. "Will it be a painful breakup for them as well?" Ryan's parents liked me. My parents weren't quite as enamored with him, but they were always courteous.

"No, they never met her. In fact, I don't think I ever really mentioned her except to tell them my girlfriend would be here for Christmas." I had no idea what he was thinking about, but I could have sworn a light went off behind his eyes.

"You must not talk to your parents much. I get an interrogation each time I call home." It starts off with *how are you* and moves into *who are you seeing*. "In my case, they were relieved when I broke up with Ryan. They always felt he wasn't the guy for me. I knew that to be the truth too, but I had worked my way into a corner and felt stuck."

It was obvious by the tilt of his head and the way his lips opened to speak that he had questions.

"Tell me about him." He leaned forward in the booth, imitating my body language. He was either interested or excelled in people skills. I imagined it was the latter. I wasn't that interesting.

"Not much to tell. I went to work at his firm. I was naïve; he was naughty. I was smitten; he was sensual. I fell, and he let me tumble. Two years later another young, smitten design student came to take my place in every way."

Most people were happy to talk about themselves. I was no different. However, this wasn't something I wanted to rehash. It was in my past, and I was over it.

"Sounds like an asshole." He tossed his napkin on the table along with two twenties. "Are you ready to go?

We've got presents to buy." He offered me his hand and pulled me from the booth. I liked the way my hand filled his, the way his fingers folded protectively around mine. Every alarm I had in my body was blaring. No good could come from liking Elias Cole.

CHAPTER 4

In the crisp morning air, we walked from boutique to boutique. Elias had no spending limit, so I was given free rein. There was a particular kind of joy that came from limitless spending. I was giddy with it, but I wondered what limitless meant to him? Certainly, everyone had a limit.

"Tell me about your sister." His face sank immediately.

"You're not going to make me come up with a sitcom character that resembles her, are you?" He fidgeted with the bags in his hands. He had purchased a beautiful silk scarf for his mom, and a cashmere sweater for his father.

"No, just tell me if she's older or younger than you." I leaned against a counter filled with Limoges boxes. "Is she married or single? What's her favorite color? What does she do for a living? Things like that." I turned and started to rifle through the tiny boxes. Who didn't love Limoges?

"No idea about the color. She seems to wear pink a lot." Looking over my shoulder toward the boxes, he continued, "She's younger by five years. She's single, and she's an accountant."

"Yuck. Boring. Not your sister, but accounting. I nearly fall asleep balancing my checkbook." There were so many beautiful boxes to choose from but I selected three, a Christmas tree, a wrapped present, and a suitcase. "Where does your family live?"

"They live in Park City, Utah." He analyzed the boxes in my hands. I handed him two of the three and reached over the table to grab a box that had a pair of skis on top. They were all beautiful, but he had to choose. Personal gifts meant so much more.

I took the boxes from his hands and lined them up on the table along with the two I had. "Pick one, then we'll get something to put in it. Maybe earrings or a necklace. You choose while I start looking at jewelry."

He looked like I'd just asked him to choose between smallpox and leprosy. Choosing a box wasn't quite so ominous. It was a simple choice. All he needed to do was close his eyes and pick one, so I left him alone, certain he could figure it out.

Within minutes he was back at my side with another bag in his hand. "I got it, I chose the gift box. It seemed the best option if we are going to put something in it."

Pragmatic. I liked that. "Good choice. What do you think of this?" I dangled a chain with a gold pine cone hanging from it in front of his face. "It's a good reminder of her time in Aspen. By the way, what's your sister's name?"

"Gretchen." He took the pine cones and stared at it from every angle. I couldn't read his expression. Wasn't sure if he liked the idea or hated it. Maybe he needed more options.

"How about a G?" I slid my arm through his and pulled him toward a different jewelry cabinet.

"Naw, this is perfect." He handed the pine cones to the salesgirl and whipped out his Amex card. "She knows how to spell her name."

We moved to the next shop—an outdoor store. It seemed the perfect playground for an active family. Elias's eyes lit up like the topper on his Christmas tree.

"Tell me who would love this store." I had hoped he would say his dad, but it was obvious Elias loved it as well.

"My dad and I used to go fly fishing when I was younger." Trance-like, he walked toward the section containing poles and nets. Describing the different flies and what they achieved, it was clear this grown man got all excited over fishhooks that looked like bugs. They had names only men could have made up. Stimulator, Prince Nymph, and San Juan Worm to name a few. We found a sturdy gray tackle box and began to fill it up with various bug-like hooks.

"You should go fishing again with your dad." I picked up a red feathery fly called a Double D. *Men.* "A fishing trip would be a great present. The gift of time is priceless." He rubbed his fingers along his clean-shaven jaw.

"I should. I miss those times." He reached over my head to grab the angler's basket hanging from the display. When he brushed against me, I inhaled the scent of him. He smelled so damn sexy. "Anyway, I got busy, and we live so far away."

"You're one state away, and the last time I checked they hadn't locked down the borders." His eyes turned soft with a look of longing, and I wondered how long it had been since he'd taken the time to be with his dad. "No excuses. It sounds like you have a good relationship with your family. Don't let it slip away because you aren't paying attention." If money hadn't been an issue I'd be with my family right now.

"You're right. I have no excuse, except work. I live, eat, and breathe work." He took his collection of flies and fishing gear to the counter and paid. "Speaking of eating, I'm starving. All this shopping builds an appetite." He seemed rather pleased with himself. Like a kid who had colored between the lines for the first time. *Did he have to be so cute too?*

"Sounds good; I'm hungry, too." It was hard for me to believe he was hungry after watching him eat a six-pound omelet just hours ago, but we had walked a long distance, and my stomach was grumbling.

We walked the packages back to the car and trotted off empty-handed for lunch and round two of shopping.

Elias picked an Italian bistro. I didn't have the heart to tell him I'd eaten Italian the night before. It didn't matter to me. I was enjoying my time with him. Becca, his ex, was an idiot. Elias was a catch. Everything about him was attractive. He bathed, he worked, he had manners, *and* he was hot.

We sat in a little booth in the corner and enjoyed breadsticks and a glass of wine while the waiter put in our order for cannelloni and lasagna.

"So, what about you? Did you get all your shopping finished?" Watching his mouth as he spoke, I decided he had lips wasted on a man. For that matter, he had eyelashes any girl would envy. Why was it the female species of the earth were saddled with dullness, while the male species were bathed in beauty? Life wasn't fair.

"Yes, I finished weeks ago. I'm not a fan of last-minute shopping. It seems disrespectful to me. Presents shouldn't be an afterthought." I didn't mean for that to sound so harsh, but I believed when you waited until the last minute, two things happened: you had to settle for what was left, and often you had to spend a whole lot more.

"How can buying a gift be considered disrespectful? It's a gift." He had a point, but . . .

"Look what we got your family so far. The scarf for your mom is lovely, and according to you, she will be overjoyed with it. It's not a gift card or a candle." I tore a breadstick into bite-sized pieces. "Your sister will appreciate the quality of the box and necklace, but the gift for your dad means something."

"My dad will love that gift." Little Elias Cole was back, and he was coloring in the lines again. He was so cute when he smiled from the heart.

"Yes. It will strike an emotion. It will conjure a memory. That's important. I knew my relationship was headed in the wrong direction last May when my ex bought me a box of business cards for my birthday. I already had two full sets in my desk drawer. He was checking off a box, filling an obligation." The memory of that day no longer brought tears to my eyes, but I had cried a river big enough for Elias and his father to fish in.

"Ouch. I have to confess. I hadn't shopped for Becca yet. We didn't have that kind of relationship." He swirled the dark red liquid in his glass. "Her job kept her out of town most weeks and mine kept me too busy to notice." He sipped his wine thoughtfully.

Hmm, I have found a flaw in Mr. Tall, Dark, and Dreamy. Is that why she strayed? Was he not invested in their relationship? He hadn't noticed her absence. Ryan had been like that, and I had hated his ambivalence.

The waiter placed our dishes in front of us. His was a meaty lasagna and mine was ricotta-filled cannelloni with marinara sauce. We would both need a mint when finished. The garlic was heavy, just the way I liked it.

"Breakups around the holidays are the worst. I'm sorry for yours." I cut into my cannelloni and watched the cheese ooze onto my plate. Breakups were a lot like cannelloni. You tried to get a clean break, but it was often messy.

"I'm not. We had two things in common. Our love for food and . . ." His ears turned red. It wasn't tough to deduce what the second thing was. "The hardest thing is disappointing my parents. I've been single for so long. I'm surprised they haven't had an intervention. Last year my sister teased me about having a coming-out party." He bit into his lasagna, and I swear I heard him hum.

"You do have a good-looking boyish face." I reached over and plucked at his heavy bottom lip. His reflexes were too quick for me. He nipped at the tip of my finger, and I squealed.

"I'm a good-looking boy? I'd like to show you how man-like I could be. I promise I could change your impression of me." A funny gasp left my mouth before I could catch it. My heart flipped like a tossed pizza. He was flirting with me . . . and I liked it.

"I was just pointing out the fact you have what I call an evergreen face. You look younger than you are, and that's a good thing. I wasn't attacking your manhood." *Nice save, Cici.*

"Too bad." Now he was just being a brat. He ran his tongue along his bottom lip, and I stared at him in the same way a cat watches a mouse. Only, I didn't pounce. I wanted to, but Elias was my boss, and I had traveled that muddy path once before.

I tried to change the subject to a neutral topic. His talk about manhood and promises had me squirming uncomfortably in my seat. It had been half a year since I'd been intimate with a man. Elias wasn't my normal type, which is why he was so perfect for me. My type only led to heartache and pain.

"We still have to get a few more things for your mom and sister. How's our budget?" I didn't want to break the bank while being his personal shopper. Lots of people said money wasn't an issue, only to panic when the credit card came.

"Really? We're fine, but I appreciate the concern. Not many women would think about the budget."

"You're hanging out with the wrong women."

"Apparently." He scrunched his napkin and covered his empty plate. The man could sure put away the food.

We walked a little slower throughout the afternoon. A nap would have been nice after all the food we'd eaten.

My favorite bookstore, Doodles, was to our right. It always called to me. There weren't many brick and mortar bookstores left in the world. They were dying a slow death due to the popularity of digital media. I liked to have a book in my hand at times, but I also liked the convenience of a Kindle. "Does your sister like to read? There's nothing better than a bubble bath and an e-reader filled with romance novels." I stared at the window display, which was packed with a book called *Twenty Dates to Love.*

"Yep, her nose is always in a book. What's a Kindle?" How could this man not know what a Kindle was?

"It's an electronic book. Call your mom and ask if Gretchen has one." I left him to make the call and walked next door into Suds, a wonderful store full of bath salts, essential oils, and bath bubbles. I was out of my bath salts and nothing relaxed me more than soaking in a tub infused with lavender.

He whispered in my ear. "What did you get?" Having not heard him approach, I nearly dropped the jar of purple salts. What a mess that would have made had it hit the tile floor and shattered. The man was lethal. His whispered words sent a chill down my spine.

I spun around and held the jar beneath his nose. He inhaled, and I could almost see the scent moving through him. He had the look of a crack addict getting his fix. First, his eyes rolled slightly backward, then his body shuddered. I imagined he would have melted into a puddle if we weren't in public.

"It's my favorite." I've always liked lavender. It had been my version of Prozac when knee-deep in finals at college.

"Now it's mine." He took the jar from my hand. He reached behind me and pulled two more from the shelf before he walked the jars to the counter and asked the saleswoman for complementary products. She came back with soaps and lotions and sachets. I pulled my jar from the mix, but he insisted on buying my bath goodies. He wouldn't take no for an answer. I hoped the women in his family liked lavender. They were getting an immense collection. I gave him credit for trying.

"What did your mom say about the Kindle?" He carried the heavy bags while I led us into several more shops.

"She said Gretchen's Kindle died several months ago. I looked them up and ordered one to be shipped overnight. Do you have a Kindle?" He pushed me toward a men's clothing store.

"I do, an older model, but it works perfectly. I hope you got her the backlit one."

"I got her the best one they had, and a gift card to fill it up."

"Ebenezer, how you've changed. And it didn't take three ghosts to pull you from the abyss."

"No, it took a Christmas elf named Chloe. What else do we need to get?" A large, genuine smile graced his gorgeous face. The look in his eyes—one of kind appreciation—should be banned. *Too* handsome. Damn the man.

"Wrapping paper, ribbons, and bows. You have a lot of wrapping to do tonight." I spun around and headed back the way we'd come. Pips Paper and Things was in the opposite direction we were walking.

"Oh no, you don't, you have to wrap too. I don't wrap. I pay people to wrap." We walked into Pips. "Oh Holy Night" serenaded the shoppers. I loved Christmas music, always had, which made it my favorite time of year to shop.

"You hired me to shop not wrap." In spite of the endless choices, I managed to narrow it down to six and asked Elias to choose four. So far he had done pretty well for a self-proclaimed Grinch. I was pretty sure choosing wrapping paper wasn't going to send him over the edge.

"Just four?" He pulled his selections from the pile. "That was easy. Now for the hard part. Will you wrap them for me?"

"No."

"No?" I didn't realize a person's brows could lift nearly to their hairline. Elias probably didn't hear that word often.

"No, I won't do it for you. I'll do it with you. Come on, Elias, you've done so well today. Dive into the whole experience. Let's go to the store and get eggnog. We can listen to Christmas music and make your packages pretty, or we can watch something on TV while we wrap."

There was no shin kicking or ear pulling and yet the man looked pained. This wasn't the firing squad. It was present wrapping.

"The last Christmas movie I watched was *Home Alone.*" His hands were full, so when we approached the register, rather than put the bags down, he asked me to reach into his pocket and grab his credit card. It seemed such a familiar thing to do.

That meant leaning into his personal space—*shame*—smelling his heavenly scent—*double shame*—and placing my hand in his pockets. *Did someone just turn the tempera-ture up in this store?*

"McCauley Caulkin is older than you. You're so far behind on Christmas movies." The cashier ran the card and Elias asked me to sign for him. I was used to signing for clients, but normally they weren't present when I spent their money. "Here's the deal. I'll help you wrap presents, but you have to watch a Christmas movie while we do it."

"Ah, Cici, you're too good to me. What would I do without you?"

"Thank goodness you don't have to figure that out. Although, I'm pretty sure you could google gift wrapping." The inside of his SUV now looked as though Kris Kringle had paid a visit. *That* had been fun.

"Cici, I appreciate what you're doing. You've been like a girlfriend for hire today. Best money I've ever spent." This morning he was all tight-gripped and white-knuckled. Now, his hands hung loosely from the steering wheel while his thumbs tapped out the beat to the song playing on the radio: "Little Drummer Boy." There may be hope for him yet.

"I'd be charging a lot more if I was your girlfriend for hire. Look at you. You're high maintenance. I've got to do everything for you."

"Ha ha, very funny."

The click of the blinker surprised me. We didn't need to turn into his driveway for another mile. When he pulled over the side of the road I began to look for emergency flashers, animals on the road, even a snowplow. Nothing.

"You're a genius. Cici, you've just solved all of my problems. You can't be home for the holidays, and I need a girlfriend. Will you be mine just until my parents leave? I'll pay you whatever you want."

He was serious. I couldn't even blame it on alcohol. We drank our wine hours ago. "Are you insane?"

"Maybe. I'm insanely intent on making sure my family has a good holiday. This will be our first one together in a few years. Please say yes. I really need you. I don't know how to do this Christmas thing."

I remember going to the pound one time and looking into the eyes of the cutest puppy. I swear it was pleading with me to save it from its uncertain future. Of course, I adopted the little, naked mole rat, a Chihuahua named Lucky. The little bastard bit me every day for a week before I sent him to a no-kill shelter.

"I'm not a girlfriend for hire. Girlfriend implies a lot. There is a certain behavior expected when two people are in a relationship, even if it's a fake one. Besides, why would you want to lie to your parents?"

Oh no, this is where I get into trouble. When the chin drops to the chest, the shoulders slump, and I can see the sparkle of hope dim in his eyes, I'm a goner. I'm not good at saying no. It's what got me into trouble the last time.

"I'm not trying to lie to my parents. I'm trying to please them. Becca was going to be in town for Christmas. I don't know how it came up. I was talking to my mom and she asked me about women. I said the woman I'm dating would be here when they arrived."

Sitting in the car in thirty-something degree weather wasn't the best place to talk about pretend relationships. If the police were to come, they'd probably think we were two teenagers making out with the amount of condensation on the windows.

"She's not here, and they're going to have to deal with it." I yanked my shirtsleeve down so it covered my hand and wiped at the clouded glass. I was feeling like the world was closing in on me. Stuck in the SUV with Elias was fine. Stuck in the SUV with Elias asking me to be his fake girlfriend was too much.

He leaned forward and hitched up the defroster. In a matter of seconds, the windows were clear, and we were moving toward his house again.

"I'm sorry I asked. It was a thought. A selfish one." He reached forward and turned the defroster down. It was hard to talk or hear over the whir of the fan. "We get along, and I thought it would be a great arrangement for both of us. You could have used the income, and I could have used the help. You did such a great job on my house. I imagined you could figure a way to finesse my parents. They would have loved you. You're exactly who they would have chosen for me."

You're exactly who they would have chosen for me. I didn't expect to hear that. What was he saying? Does he like me or does he simply think I'm good girlfriend material . . . someone his parents would approve of but not necessarily him? Elias Cole is one confusing man. Sweet, but confusing.

"That's very sweet, but it's not going to help your case." It made me wonder whom he chose for himself. Was he like me and became blind and stupid when it came to the opposite sex?

My ex was handsome and attentive. He'd dressed nice, smelled nice, and drove a nice car. Love had to be more than *nice*. I wasn't going to settle for nice again. My version of nice sent me off to work while he stayed at the office and banged the second assistant. There's nothing worse than finding your man with another woman. Now that woman lived in my house in Brentwood. She can have him. Sadly, she might end up just as hurt as me.

Elias wasn't offering me a real relationship. His offer was an acting assignment. I may have acted impulsively when I said no. Maybe it wouldn't be such a bad idea to consider his offer. I did need the money, and his motives came from a good place.

We rounded the corner and pulled into the garage. I'd never entered the house from here. It was like seeing it for the very first time. The garage led into a massive entertainment room. Huge TVs hung from the wall in various locations; a pool table was off to the side. The focal point of the room was definitely the bar. It was large enough to seat eight, looked like it was hand carved, and appeared to be fully stocked.

"I'll get the bags. Open a bottle of whatever wine you want to share." He headed back to the garage.

What an incredible stock of wine. A connoisseur? I pulled out the Duck Horn Cabernet and dusted it off. The corkscrew sat on the counter like it was waiting for me. After pulling the cork, I set the bottle aside to let the wine breathe.

While Elias brought in the bags, I organized the gifts by recipient. It was a good way to see what he had for each person, and it allowed us to ensure one person didn't end up with all red paper.

After Elias poured us a glass of wine, we sat in the center of the floor surrounded by gifts and paper.

"What movie are we watching? It was part of the agreement." He fell back on the carpet and lay prone. If I weren't so polite, I would have tickled the part of his stomach that peeked out below his shirt. The part that showed his happy trail dipping below his pants. *Focus, Cici.*

"Let's see what's on the tube." He sat up and, to my disappointment, pulled his shirt down. Too bad. He clicked through the stations with rapid-fire reflexes. The pictures passed so fast I couldn't process anything.

"Slow down." He stopped pressing buttons when *The Grinch Who Stole Christmas* came on. *Perfect.* "I love this show. I always dreamed of being a Who from Whoville. I made my mom call me Chloe Lou Who for an entire Christmas break."

"All right, Chloe Lou Who, where do we start?" He gave me a smile that had the perfect mixture of mischief and sensuality. It was almost too hard to ignore. But I did.

"Mom's first, then we'll move down the line." The rectangular box holding the scarf would be easy. We would move on to the tougher stuff later.

He caught on right away. I'm not sure he *needed* me to wrap the gifts. However, I got the distinct impression he didn't want to be alone. His family was arriving tomorrow, and maybe he needed reassurance everything would be fine. It had, after all, been years since they'd celebrated together.

"Nice, huh?" He held up the perfectly wrapped box for me to see.

"Yes, good job." I tossed him the box that contained the lambskin gloves for his sister. I started on his father's box of feather bugs. I never understood the thrill people got from fishing. They came with that slimy stuff all over their bodies for a reason. Fish were the greased pigs of the water.

"Tell me more about yourself. What do you do for fun?" He turned the paper around and pulled too tight. *Rrrrip.* The corner of the package tore while he attempted to get a wrinkle out. "Damn, I messed this one up. I told you I shouldn't wrap."

I handed him a new sheet from the pile and told him to begin again. He wasn't getting out of wrapping presents.

He turned to me with his sad face again. Oh, even the man's pout was sexy. Nice try, Elias. Nice try.

"I like to hike. Not mountain hike, but nature hike.

I'm a good swimmer, having grown up by the beach, and I love books in a way that can't be healthy." I wasn't that interesting. Maybe that's why I was thirty and still single.

"Explain." He placed a bow on the corner of his perfectly wrapped box. I was impressed when he criss-crossed two candy canes and taped them in place. His eyes kept glancing at the TV where the Whos were decorating the tree in Whoville.

"I'm trying to get through Time Magazine's 100 all-time best novels. I'm on number eleven. I started last year. I figure I'll read one a month from the list. Add that to my one or two a week from my Kindle collection, and you can see I'm addicted to words."

"Reading is a worthwhile hobby." He reached for the next present, the sweater for his father. "Do you prefer the Kindle?" He grabbed the green-foiled paper and went to work.

"Unless I'm collecting hardbacks like the top 100, then yes, I prefer my digital reader." Currently, I was reading Darynda Jones's Charley Davidson series. I'd never get enough of Reyes Farrow and his unholy hotness. "Anyway, an e-reader is convenient. I can carry thousands of books with me everywhere, and it weighs less than a pound."

"I can see the benefit. So, is that what you'll be doing the next few days? Reading?"

The sad answer was yes, but at least I didn't have a houseful of cats. It was Jax and me. "I'm sure I'll talk to my family. As you already know I love Christmas movies, and there's sure to be a marathon of them. Then there's Macy's parade." We were moving through the presents quickly. Partnerships always made things go more smoothly, and we made a good team.

"I wish you would reconsider my offer." He reached for my glass to top off my wine. I liked the way he saw to my needs. That was a nice trait in a man. He would make some girl very happy.

"Elias—"

"Cici, hear me out. You're alone for the holidays, and I have too much family to handle. It's just three of them, but they can wear me out. We don't have to introduce you as my girlfriend. In fact, I won't use the G-word once while they're here. If they assume you are . . ." His shoulders rose in a *so what* fashion. "You can stay in the room next to mine. I'll put them on the opposite side of the house."

"Why is this so important to you? Please don't tell me your mother is terminal." *God, don't let him tell me someone in his family is dying.*

Once he stopped laughing, he continued. "No one is dying. Well, my mother is dying for me to meet someone, fall in love, and give her grandbabies, but other than that, they're all healthy."

"Glad to hear it."

"What can I say to make you change your mind?" He tilted his head like the sad puppies in those SPCA ads that made me cry.

I was a sucker for sad eyes.

I didn't want to spend Christmas alone. Jax was cute, but how pentertaining could a goldfish be? "Please. You could say please." It took him a minute to digest my answer. I'm not sure he was certain he'd heard correctly. He continued to tilt his head like a confused puppy.

"Did you actually say yes?"

"Yes."

He flew from the floor, pulled me into his strong arms, and twirled me in circles. The scene was straight out of a movie, only the hero had just proposed, and the heroine had said yes.

When his arms dropped to his sides I felt the loss. If anything, being his fake girlfriend should guarantee me a few more hugs, but he wouldn't be expecting more than that. Would he?

"That's amazing. Now we have to go to dinner and negotiate your salary. We have so many things to learn about each other. You can't be my girl—I mean with me—and not know certain things."

There were three additional gifts to wrap, and the bath salts hadn't surfaced yet. He must have left them in the car.

"Where are the bath salts?" I gave the room a once-over, wondering if they'd been set elsewhere.

"I'll wrap them later, along with the rest of these. We have to go. We have so much to do." He pulled me toward the door. I barely had time to reach out and grab my coat and bag. He had me in the car so fast we could have produced a safety video on how to exit your house in seconds.

"Why the rush? Your parents come in tomorrow."

"Yes, but early tomorrow so we need to be up and ready by eight. That gives us very little time to move your clothes and stuff to my house."

"Why can't we say I live in Aspen, and then I can stay at my apartment? I don't like lying. I'm not a dishonest person."

"You don't have to lie. My mom isn't going to ask you where you live. She'll assume you stay with me. She's a forward thinker."

"Okay, tell me the things I need to know." He began to tell me his life story as we drove down the mountain into town. By the time he pulled in front of The Jazz Cafe, I felt like I'd watched a movie on the biography channel. He played football in school and was an honor student. He went to Denver University, which is how he ended up in Colorado. He has a gnarly scar on his ankle from a bicycle accident. He doesn't like lentils. He hates eating fish of any kind, which is ironic given his love for the sport.

He also had great taste in restaurants. He managed to choose two of my favorite locations in the same day. We were seated right away and both ordered burgers. His was something called a black and blue which sounded painful. Mine was a protein-packed black bean burger.

"Tell me about you." He sipped on his soda.

"What exactly do you want to know? You already know my hobbies. I have a passion for interior design. I have a pet fish." At the mention of Jax his nose turned. "You know what I drive, and that I was born and raised in California."

"What size do you wear?" *What the?* Inquisitive minds want to know the weirdest stuff.

"Why?"

"Because my mom will want to get you something while we're out, and she'll ask me. Any man worth his weight knows everything about his woman." He sat back self-assured and smug.

"I'm not your woman." The server delivered our meals. Elias dug into his. Throughout the day he had eaten enough to feed a small country. I suppose it took a lot of calories to support those muscles. And, let's be honest, I wasn't complaining.

"You are for the next several days. Speaking of which, I intend to pay your hourly rate twenty-four hours a day. I won't argue with you."

That was twelve hundred dollars a day. A lot of money to pay for what he was getting in the bargain. A whole lot of nothing. "What are your expectations? I'll be able to prepare better if I know what I'm up against."

"Just be yourself. Enjoy my family and the house you decorated. We'll go skiing, eat out a lot, and enjoy each other."

I wasn't going to argue with him. I needed the money, and he needed me. It seemed like a fair trade. "Sounds reasonable." I wondered if there would be any kissing. I could go for some kissing. "How am I supposed to act around you? Am I totally in love with you, or are we still establishing the groundwork for our relationship?" I chewed the end of my fry until it was a nub between my fingers.

"How does totally in love look?" He licked the grease that spilled over his lip. Everything in my body shuddered. How could this man make me quake with a simple glimpse of his tongue?

"I could hang on your every word. I could sit at your feet and gaze longingly into your eyes. I could constantly whisper naughty things in your ear. My hands could seek you all day," I purred. "You know, stuff like that." It was funny to watch his face turn pink as I cooed my answers to him.

"I could go for the naughty whispers and touching. I'm

not sure about the rest. Why don't we strive for something in between?" He wiped his mouth and tossed his napkin on his plate. "Handholding and a peck on the cheek could make it seem real. We would still be at the I-want-to-please stage of our relationship." Was that hard for him to say, given his girlfriend had just left him? Unlike me, she wasn't a people pleaser.

"Shouldn't people be at that stage throughout the entire relationship? Relationships fail because people get lazy or greedy." I'd barely eaten anything. I was too consumed with my new job to focus on food. "I'm sorry, but I heard some of your conversation with Becca. I wasn't eavesdropping; I thought you'd hurt yourself, and I was coming to help."

A pained expression crossed his face. "So you heard me talking about him?"

Feeling ashamed I had stayed long enough to have heard that much, I lowered my head in embarrassment and nodded. "I heard a little." I heard it all, but what purpose did it serve to repeat it?

"Becca is a chef. She cooks for a family. A wealthy widower and his children. She informed me she was cooking up something extra on the side, and it turns out it wasn't happening in the kitchen." As he spoke he didn't seem upset, and I wondered where the pained expression had come from.

"I'm sorry, Elias. You deserve more." My hand slid across the table and reached for his. He folded my hand in his and nodded.

"You know what hurts the most? It's not that she left me. We'd only been together for several months, but we'd only seen each other a handful of times. If I'm honest, it hurt my ego. She left me for an older man with three kids."

"Idiot. She was obviously an idiot." I liked the way he opened up to me. Not many men would admit to having an ego, much less a bruised one.

"I'm not sure she knows what she wants. It's probably not anywhere near what I want, so the breakup was for the better."

"What do you want, Elias?" What did a man like him want? Marriage? Children? Maybe he wanted none of those things, and Becca couldn't see a future with him.

"Now that I'm financially secure, I want to settle down." He looked around the restaurant and his sight lingered on the families. "I want a partner in life and a family of my own." I hadn't realized we were still holding hands until he let go of mine.

"Why would she take on a pre-made family if she was with a man who was looking to have one with her? It doesn't make sense." I wanted to reach over and drag his hand back to mine. I liked the feel of his warm palm encasing my hand.

"We didn't get that far in our talks. I know Becca wanted kids but was scared to death of the whole pregnancy thing. She used three types of birth control to make sure she didn't end up pregnant. The pill, an IUD, and condoms. A bit overkill, don't you think? It made me feel like my come was radioactive." He seemed a bit exasperated by the whole ordeal. The way he described it gave me a picture of Becca suiting up in a Hazmat suit before entering the bedroom. I struggled to hold back a giggle.

"Now you can look for the woman who wants what you want." What kind of woman would turn Elias's head?

Would she be high-maintenance and glamorous? A skier with an athletic build? Obviously, he liked to eat, so Becca being a chef had to have been a bonus.

He looked at me thoughtfully, the way a man looks at something he's trying to figure out. "What do you want, Cici?" He slid from the booth and helped me stand. With my jacket in his hands, he held it open as I slid my arms inside. He was a gentleman. A rare breed these days.

"I want it all. I want a husband, a family, and a career." *You. I'd want you.* "Unfortunately, I'm getting up in years and the family part is slipping past me." At thirty I felt I had very few childbearing years left and, with no love interest in sight, things were looking grim in that department.

"You sound like you've given up. Never give up. Love could be around the corner. Keep your eyes open." He sounded like an ad for a dating website.

Maybe I needed the book in the bookstore window, *Twenty Dates to Love.* Oh, who was I kidding? I couldn't get a real date, let alone twenty. Hell, a man who would make an amazing real boyfriend was hiring me as a fake girlfriend. Life could be so cruel.

After Elias paid our bill, he guided me to his car. Within fifteen minutes we were at my place. It wasn't much. I rented a one-room studio, so everything was in one spacious room. Fabric hanging from the ceiling divided the living spaces. It had a bohemian-loft feel to it. Very different from Elias's mountain home. My entire living space would fit in his great room.

"This is the coolest place ever." He walked past me into my living room. I had a sofa, flanked by overstuffed chairs. Panels of draperies hung from the ceiling on three sides. The rich earth tones created a cocoon of sorts. It was cozy and inviting.

I swelled with pride. This man saw million-dollar homes every day, and he thought my little pad was cool. "Glad you like it. I'll pack up some things to take to your house. We have to take Jax too." I pointed to the fishbowl on the coffee table. "Make yourself comfortable while I get ready."

I heard the TV click on as soon as I pushed past the curtains into my bedroom space. The unmistakable script of National Lampoon's Christmas Vacation played in the background. He was watching the part where Clark was turning on the Christmas lights for the first time.

I tuned it out and started packing. Would his parents like me? Did it matter? Of course not, this wasn't real. I would do what was asked of me. And come next week, I'd be looking for another job to pay my bills. Making ends meet week to week and month to month would be my new norm until I could establish myself. I hated to live that way. I'd worked my ass off so I didn't have to and yet . . .

I came across my ski pants. "You're not going to make me ski, are you?" I called from my room, hoping he would say no. I was in no hurry to embarrass myself in front of his family. I wasn't the cute ski bunny who barreled down the hill and came to a perfect snow-spraying stop. I was the girl whose limbs flailed about while she tried to dodge the ski school and failed, knocking them down like perfectly placed dominoes.

His voice so close behind me made me jump. "Yes, I'll get you an instructor to help with your form. It's one of the perks of your temporary job."

I spun around and found him settling in on my bed. I hadn't heard him approach, but damn he looked good *there*.

"Gave up on the Christmas show?" There had to be a reason for his disinterest in Christmas. A reason I planned to squeeze from someone over the next few days. There was no way I could be in a relationship with someone, fake or not, who didn't absolutely love the holidays.

"Yes, this seemed more interesting." He lay on his back and brought his arms up behind his head. He took up two-thirds of my bed.

"Oh, brother. I can't believe you'd rather watch me pack my underwear than watch Clark Griswold light up his house." I began to set my things in piles on the bed.

"I'd love to see your underwear. We're a couple, and I've never seen them yet. A shame, don't you think?" He was lying on my bed flirting. Lord, this was going to be a long week.

I threw my flannel pajamas at his head. "This is as close to my undies as you're going to get."

He held up the flannel PJs decorated with penguins on skis. "Please don't tell me this is what you wear to bed. No wonder you don't have a boyfriend. Why would you hide that," his hand did a perfect Vanna White in front of my body, "in those?" He pointed back to the pajamas I had neatly folded and set on the bed. "You have an incredible body. Show it off." As soon as he said that, he bit into his bottom lip.

Embarrassment looked adorable on him. He was this interesting mix of strength and innocence. He also had good taste—he thought I had an incredible body. Imagine that.

How could I explain my love of flannel? "It's winter, and it's cold, and for your information, when I'm in a relationship I don't wear anything to bed. It's up to my significant other to keep me warm." I waited for his face to turn red, but it didn't. He looked me up and down like he had X-ray vision. Dressed fully, I'd never felt so exposed. *Fuck. Me.* Don't look at me like that, Mr. Cole.

Under his watchful eye, I packed the rest of my clothes, including my ski gear. He loaded my bag into the car while I grabbed my bathroom items. When he returned, he looked at my Charlie Brown tree in the corner and laughed. The man laughed.

"What? It's a cute tree." I tried to slug him in the arm for teasing my tree, but he was too quick. He grabbed my arm and pulled me into his chest. This was the second time he'd hugged me today.

"It's a cute something. Not sure if I can call it a tree." His hand skimmed up and down my back. "Thanks, Cici, for doing this for me. I want to have a great holiday without my parents worrying about me spending the rest of my life alone."

"You're welcome. I can't wait to meet your family. They are obviously important enough for you to go to the extreme." I swear he brushed his lips against my hair. My scalp tingled where I imagined his lips touched.

"I'll grab your presents from under the tree. We'll bring them to the house." He separated himself from me and walked to the little decorated branch in the corner. He was only ten feet away, but I felt the loss the minute he let me go. His presence hugged me, and his absence hollowed me.

His muscles flexed as he piled the presents into his

arms. It hadn't occurred to me to take the gifts along, but I'm glad he thought of it. My mom would be calling Christmas morning to see if I liked whatever she'd made.

Whatever it was, I would cherish it, as she would have put hours of love into what she'd created. By the weight of the box, I'd bet it was a hat, a scarf, or something I could wear.

Over my shoulder, I looked at my home. Despite its tiny size, I was proud of my apartment. Proud of my accomplishment to stay despite the challenges in finding work. It hadn't been easy, but I felt I'd found my independence.

Jax sloshed in the bowl I carried to my car. I expected to spend my first Christmas in Colorado alone. Instead, I was heading up the mountain to pretend I was the cherished girlfriend of a handsome man, trying to please his family. I wished Elias Cole was mine.

The smell of coffee woke me from my deep sleep. I was tucked in the pillow-top mattress of Elias's guest room bed. It had been tough falling asleep with him so close.

The air crackled with energy, and I was no longer alone. Elias stood above me shirtless in his flannel pajama bottoms. Had I died and gone to Chippendales?

"You need to wake up. We have to leave in an hour. The housekeeper is downstairs. She'll take care of your bed. It's sheet cleaning day." He placed a cup of steaming coffee on the nightstand next to the bowl where Jax happily swam. "I can make tea if you prefer. Just thought you might need the hit of caffeine."

I don't think I've ever had someone bring me coffee in bed. This was a morning ritual I could get used to.

Self consciously, I ran my fingers through my hair knowing my curls would be everywhere. I wasn't ready for him to see me like this. I opened my mouth, but nothing came out. His naked chest silenced me. The man obviously worked out. I was tempted to reach up and touch the curly hairs sprinkled across his chest. Would they be soft or prickly? My fingers were itching to know, but I refrained. Too intimate.

"Thanks, coffee is perfect," I whispered from behind the hand I placed in front of my mouth. No sense in accosting him with morning breath. My eyes traveled down his torso to rest on his red plaid pants. "And you gave me a hard time about my flannels?"

Inching up against the headboard, I settled against the soft fabric and took in the sight in front of me. A shadow of whiskers took away his boyish looks and replaced them with a roguishly handsome man.

"I don't normally wear anything, Cici, but I thought you might appreciate it if I covered up."

"Don't think so hard next time." Holy shit. I just gave him permission to visit me nude. What was I thinking?

The sound of his laughter filled my room while he walked toward the door. The red plaid of his pajamas hugged the perfect globes of his perfect ass. An ass I'd love to get my hands on.

The covers fell from the bed when I tossed them to the side. I had to get a grip on myself. This week would be a disaster if I continued to fawn over him like a lovesick teenager. Or maybe that would work in my favor. My attraction to him would certainly play into our whole couple charade. I wouldn't need to feign interest. I was genuinely interested in the man. I just wished we had met under different circumstances.

Problem number one: I worked for him. That was a firm no-go in my new rulebook. Number two: he wasn't genuinely interested in me. He was paying me to pretend.

Number three: his aversion to the holiday season. If we were a real couple it would be like setting Mary Poppins up with Voldemort. That combination would never work.

After I showered and dressed, I made my way down the stairs to the kitchen. I only needed to follow the trail of his cologne to know where he was. Wouldn't he be stunned to know that his cologne reminded me of a Christmas pomander? He was a walking Christmas symbol. When I closed my eyes, I could see the oranges wrapped in ribbon and studded with cloves hanging from his Christmas tree. I breathed deeply to inhale the scent of him.

"Good morning." His deep voice vibrated through my body. Words slipped from his lips like warm pudding. Sweet. Smooth. Full of temptation. "You look beautiful."

"You don't have to start with your act yet, but I like where you're going." I twirled my finger through a curl and let it spring back into place. His words were downright delectable, and I only hoped I could perform as well.

"No act. You look beautiful. I've only seen you with your hair pulled up on top of your head. This morning it was everywhere. It's lovely." He reached out and pulled a curl through his fingers. I found myself leaning in toward his hand. He reciprocated by cupping my cheek. It felt so natural. So real or was that surreal?

"Thank you. You are looking quite handsome yourself." He was dressed in gray slacks and a lighter gray button-down shirt. No tie. Collar open. On his feet were the Italian leather loafers I'd chastised him about a few days ago. Had it really only been four days? It seemed like a lifetime.

On the counter was an array of pastries and yogurts. I

don't remember seeing those in the refrigerator, but then again it's not like I'd been living here. He must have gone shopping. With a strawberry yogurt in my hand, I sat at the granite island in the same chair I'd sat in when he'd made me an omelet. He took the chair next to me.

"Are you nervous?" He pulled the yogurt from my hand and stripped the foil lid free.

Was I nervous? "I'm meeting your parents, how could I not be?" It didn't matter our relationship was fabricated, I was still meeting his parents, and therefore I was a tad apprehensive. I'd still be scrutinized. The one thing I knew about parents was no one was ever good enough for their kid. They would be judging me first as his girlfriend and second as a human being, and I hoped I passed on at least the second category.

"They'll love you. In fact, that's going to be the real problem. They'll love you, and then they'll hate me for breaking up with you."

"Why not just tell them the truth?" I understood his need to please his family, but this was his life, and if his family was as close as I assumed, they would understand that shit happens. Including breakups with unfortunate timing.

"Grab your coat, and I'll explain in the car. We have to get on the road." He helped me into my jacket and guided me into the garage where a tiny older woman was unloading groceries from her car. Now I knew where the food had come from. He introduced me to his house-keeper, Sara, and we were on our way.

"She seems nice." I was happy to see so many bags in the car. I hadn't thought about what his family would eat while they were visiting. "Does she always shop for you?"

He had mentioned going out a lot, so I simply figured that was the plan.

"Pretty much." He made no excuses for having help. It was a perk of having money.

"How does she know what to get?" I wondered if they had a system. Did he email her? Was there a standing order she kept ready and waiting for when he arrived?

"I usually email her a list. Although this time Becca did. I'm glad she at least completed that task."

"It's a good thing. We certainly weren't thinking about food, were we?" He turned his head briefly, and I got a glimmer of something in his eye. It resembled mischievousness, and I wondered what he was thinking.

He reached over and took my hand in his. His thumb rubbed my knuckles in the most sensuous way. I nearly melted into his heated leather seat. "Seeing you in those sexy flannels this morning had me thinking all kinds of thoughts." He slowly pulled his moist tongue across his lower lip. "I was thinking about my grandmother and how you two could shop together." He let go of my hand and slapped the steering wheel in rhythm with his laughter.

"You're awful. And, obviously, your grandmother has impeccable taste. I'd love to meet her."

"She's dead."

"Shit, Elias. I'm sorry." He tapped the steering wheel harder while he cracked up beside me. That's when I reached over and punched him.

"Ouch." He rubbed at his arm while his laughter subsided. "You're too easy. I couldn't resist. Anyway, my grandmother is alive and well. She lives in Pasadena. She teaches water aerobics at the YMCA. She'll outlive us all."

"I think I hate you. You're a mean man." I glared out

the window and watched the landscape whiz by. The snow-flocked trees created the perfect winter wonderland.

"Hey, love, are we having our first argument? If so let's get it finished so we can make up. We're only twenty minutes from the airport. Can't have us at odds just yet."

I wanted to reach over and punch him again, but I settled for a growl.

"You said you would explain to me why this was so important. You better come up with a compelling reason, or I might decide to leave you." His face went from a hundred watts down to twenty. I wasn't sure I wanted to know anymore.

"The long and short of it is I used to love the holidays. Then seven years ago, I planned to propose to my girl-friend. We had been together throughout college. I took her to my parents for Christmas. I put the ring under the tree. When she opened the box she cried, and I thought it was a good thing. Nope. She turned me down flat. Said I was fine for playing not for staying. She dumped me in front of my family. She took off that afternoon and joined a cruise ship staff so she could see the world."

Oh shit. "You better not be messing with me again, Elias. If I find out you're lying, I'll slug you so hard you'll feel it in your other arm." I fisted up, ready to swing if he laughed. No laughter came.

"This time I'm serious. She broke my heart. Ruined Christmas for me and swore me off relationships. Now, Becca."

I wanted to climb across the console and hold him. Why did people have to be so cruel? Especially around the holidays. I never understood.

"Becca is a total fool. She'll be back once she realizes what an imbecile she was. What's not to love about you? You're hella-sexy, and you're successful. You obviously take your family commitments seriously, and you have a great . . ." I almost said ass, but I thought better of it. "Personality."

"I'm hella what?"

I lowered my head in embarrassment. Maybe I should have just blurted the ass part out. Honestly, it was true, and now I had to confess the sexy part, why not get it all out. But I didn't. I whispered, "sexy."

When I looked up to see his wide grin, he reached for my hand and squeezed it, and my heart, at the same time.

"We are going to have a wonderful holiday, Chloe Lou Who. You are my Christmas angel."

We pulled into the airport parking lot. Elias ran around the SUV and helped me out into the frigid winter air. Instead of pulling me toward the terminal, he pulled the collar of my jacket up around my ears and leaned down and kissed me square on the lips. Something about the kiss was so sweet and earnest. Many women had let Elias down around the holidays. I wouldn't be one of them. *I like this man.*

CHAPTER 7

My heart spun and twirled like the cymbals in a drum line. "Cici, you look petrified." He laid his arm around my shoulder and pulled me close to his body. The nicer he was, the more I realized what an idiot Becca had been to give him up. Who in their right mind would give up this man?

"It's part of my act. Shouldn't the love interest be afraid to meet the parents?" After the kiss, everything scared me. It was a peck just like he said we'd trade, but it felt too real. Obviously, it wasn't, but . . . Maybe he was just practicing as well?

"Don't stress. It'll all be fine." He pointed to the redheaded woman and gray-haired man that walked hand in hand down the concourse. "Here they come." A girl version of Elias walked about two steps behind the couple. They were all smiles, but when I looked up at Elias, his smile was gone.

Oh, great. He's nervous now?

His mother went straight for me. "You must be Elias's

girlfriend. I'm so glad to meet you. I wish I could say I knew everything about you, but Elias keeps everything so close to his vest." She pulled back and took me in. "We have several days to get to know each another." She pulled me to her and hugged me like I was a lifeline.

"Mom, let the poor girl go. The rest of us want to meet her too," the Elias with boobs said.

Pulled from his mother's arms, I was passed from relative to relative. I'd never been hugged and squeezed so much in such a short amount of time. In fact, I was even passed to strangers. An older woman squeezed my cheek and pushed me toward a man she referred to as Fritz.

I felt Elias's hands wrap around my waist. His chest came into tight contact against my back when he pulled me against him. I loved the feel of him holding me. His strong presence gave me strength.

"Now that you've accosted her and pawed her to death, maybe I should introduce her." He looked at the five people standing in front of us. "This is my Chloe, but she prefers to be called Cici."

Stuck to his chest we shuffled side by side as he made the introductions. First his mom, Maggie. The joy of seeing her son was apparent. Her eyes twinkled with the light only a proud mother could possess. Next was his dad, Clint, and finally his sister, Gretchen.

When we got to the old woman, his mother sang out, "Surprise." He introduced the woman as his grandmother, Izzy. Next in line was Uncle Fritz. Obviously, he wasn't expecting them. We would be two seats short in the car, and the house was a whole other issue.

"Definitely a surprise. Why didn't you tell me? I could

have prepared for them." He bent and whispered something in his mother's ear.

"They didn't come for presents, Elias, they came to see you and your girlfriend." There was that word Elias and I promised not to utter, and yet his family tossed it around freely.

We waited at baggage claim for their luggage. I had been claimed as well, not once did Elias let go of my hand. Growing up, I'd always welcomed handholding and hugs from my family. Ryan hadn't been a very tactile man, which had always bothered me. I hadn't realized how much I missed simple affection. *Why can't I find a man like Elias?* He continues to tick so many boxes, and his frequent touches of affection make me feel cherished. How I wish it wasn't fantasy.

We loaded everything in the SUV and the rental car Clint had reserved and then headed toward the house. Maggie and Gretchen drove with Elias and me.

"Cici, how did you meet my brother?" Gretchen reached forward and placed her hand on my shoulder. It was warm and friendly just like the woman who offered it.

Shit, that was one thing Elias and I didn't cover. I had no idea how we were going to answer the questions about our relationship. I couldn't tell the truth. That would put us meeting five days ago. I looked at Elias hoping he would save me.

"Cici is an interior designer. We met on a job." His answer was man-like: short and detail free.

Maggie was next. "I thought you said she was a chef." Maggie leaned forward. I twisted in my seat to look in her direction.

"Mom, you must have misunderstood. I said she was an excellent cook, but I never said she was a chef." Elias reached over and brushed my arm with his hand. He let it rest on top of mine, silently giving me strength.

"No, Elias, I swear you said chef because you said she was going to cook us a wonderful Christmas dinner. I know I didn't dream it." His mother looked at the back of his head like his brains would spill out. When she looked at me, I must have turned white. "Cici, are you okay? You look ill."

"Fine. I'm fine. I get a bit car sick when we drive in the mountains." I turned around and stared out the front window wondering how on God's green earth was I going to pull this off. I would have to cook a feast for his family, and I'd never eaten meat.

After a barrage of questions toward Elias and me, Maggie and Gretchen started talking to one another about the ski conditions. Elias took that opportunity and made a quick call to Sara. In a hushed voice, he gave her directions on getting the spare rooms set up for unexpected guests. Including my room, there were only two guest rooms available, and I couldn't imagine Uncle Fritz and Grandma Izzy sharing one. Someone was not going to be happy with their accommodations, and I imagined it would be me.

When we pulled up to the house, Elias didn't pull into the garage. I imagine he wanted his family to enter through the front door. He was proud of his house and would want to show it off properly.

His parents oohed and aahed over the landscaping. It turned out Clint owned a landscaping company and could appreciate the simplicity of the xeriscaping of Elias's property. There was so much I didn't know. It was as if Elias and I had just met. Hell, we had just met, and it would be obvious to everyone if we didn't get our stories straight.

When Elias opened the front door, I was filled with pride. My work on the enormous tree took center stage. Everyone was drawn to it like a bug to a light. His grandmother was the first to speak.

"That's one fine tree you have there, my boy. Who decorated it?"

Elias looked around the room until he found me standing behind his family. In seconds he was at my side with his hands on my shoulders. "Cici and I decorated the tree. She wouldn't let me help with the rest of the house, but she did allow me to assist with the tree and the gift wrapping." He brushed his lips down my cheek and nuzzled into the soft place between my shoulder and collarbone. The shiver ran from my neck to my toes.

"Elias is a fibber. I had to beg him to wrap presents, but when he got started, I found out he was quite adept at it." I looked from person to person. "Who should I thank for that?"

Gretchen raised her hand. "I used to volunteer him at church for the wrapping table. We did it for donations that ran the daycare center. He pretended he hated it, but he was always good at it."

I stepped out of his arms—reluctantly—and walked over to Gretchen to give her a high five.

"Let me show everyone their rooms, and then we'll go into town. Mom has already indicated a desire to do some shopping." Elias reached down to pick up his grandmother's and mother's bags and led the way. Fritz and Clint picked up Gretchen's heavy suitcases and grumbled while they dragged them upstairs.

I followed Elias as he showed his family their rooms. I had not seen the entire house yet. Another mistake in our planning or lack thereof. When we got to my room, my belongings were no longer present. It was like I'd never slept there.

Elias gave me a look that begged forgiveness. "Uncle Fritz, this is your room."

All I wanted to know was where was I sleeping now that I'd been evicted?

We left everyone to get settled. The plan was to meet downstairs in fifteen minutes. Elias pulled me into his room and closed the door.

His room was enormous. A massive log bed took center stage. Like my house, his was decorated in warm hues of brown, orange, gold, and beige. "What now, Einstein?" I walked around his room, stroking the top of his dresser while I moved. "We certainly didn't plan this."

"You can sleep in here. I'll sleep on the floor. No one will know." He sat in the leather chair next to the bed. "I already had Sara move your stuff into my bathroom and closet. It was the only choice I had. I'm sorry." When I reached his bed, I climbed on top. The plush duvet was soft and warm. My fingers brushed the brown velveteen of the coverlet. Exquisite.

"We're out of our minds if we think we're going to get away with this. Your mother is already suspicious. What will she think when I serve up my favorite Christmas dish, quinoa with cranberries and squash? Obviously, you haven't noticed, but I'm a vegetarian, Elias. I've never eaten nor cooked a piece of flesh in my life."

He leaned forward and let his head fall into his hands. I've never seen anyone look so defeated.

"I had no idea you didn't eat meat. That will never work. We're supposed to have prime rib for Christmas dinner. You ate eggs and cheese. Those are animal products."

"Yes, but you don't have to kill the animal to get them. I'm a lacto-ovo-vegetarian. We're not calling it off. You hired me, and I plan to complete my job. I won't be another woman who lets you down."

"Just a second ago you said we would never pull this off, and you're probably right. Let's just call it off. It's too much. It was a bad idea. I'm sorry."

"I've changed my mind." I hopped off the bed, kneeled beside him, and looked up into his worried eyes. "Let's try. I'll run into the bookstore when we get to town and grab a cookbook. How hard can cooking a cow be?" I leaned my head on his knee. I couldn't believe I was begging to cook an animal.

I didn't become vegetarianism by choice. I was raised one, and I'd never changed. There was no need. Now, there was a need. Elias needed me to come through for him. He told his mother his chef girlfriend would be here, and I would do my darnedest to help her show up. I did my best work under pressure.

"You don't need to go to extremes for me." His hand found its way into my hair. *Did he realize how intimate his touch was?* When he touched me like that, I would do anything for him. I'd throw a hoedown and barbecue an entire herd if he asked.

"Elias. Isn't it time someone went to extremes for you? I'm not the girl who turned you down seven years ago, and I'm not Becca. I'm simply the girl who wants you to fall in love with Christmas again. So, let's do this thing." I used his knees to pull myself into a standing position. Then I pulled him up, next to me. It was easy to wrap my arms around his waist. I could have stayed there all day, but we had a family to fool, and I had a dinner to plan. I pried my hands from him and turned to walk to the door.

He reached out and dragged me back. This time when his lips touched mine, it was real. His tongue probed, and I allowed him access. The kiss deepened, grew more insistent, and my body answered with a tremor of desire. His tongue dipped between my lips. He didn't just taste me, he drank me in like his thirst couldn't be quenched.

We walked together until I was trapped between him and the wall. I felt his hardness press against my hip and a spark ignited between my thighs. When I reached down to stroke him, he stepped back and spun away from me. The movement was so quick it dizzied me.

"Shit, Cici. I'm sorry. I felt . . . I felt . . . shit. Cici, I'd never take advantage of you. I'm sorry." He paced the room in front of me, looking guilty. How was I supposed to ease his conscience when mine was feeling just as bad?

I wasn't sorry he kissed me, but I was grateful he stopped. I'd almost broken my set-in-granite rules. No sleeping with the boss. Maybe I'd spoken too early when I changed my mind and decided to stay. I was beginning to feel like an addict, and Elias was my much-needed fix.

I reached up and caressed his cheek. "Elias, the kiss . . . was great, but don't worry about it." Actually, the kiss was *exceptional.* "It was just a thing that happened in the moment. We can't let the stress of the situation get the better of us. Let's forget about it. No harm done." That wasn't exactly the truth. I'd had a taste of what he had to offer, and I would always wonder what the rest would be like. All I had to say was Becca was a stupid, stupid, woman. A man who could melt your underwear with a kiss should never be overlooked.

Everyone was waiting when we emerged from the room. They all looked at us like we had stripped and jumped each other only minutes before. I blushed under their stares. Once again Elias reached for my hand and pulled me close. He seemed to know when I was feeling insecure, and I was grateful for the offered comfort.

Clint and Fritz decided to stay at home and check out the bar. The rest of us piled in the Range Rover and made our way down the mountain.

Once we reached the town, Elias broke off from the group to do some last-minute shopping. I was sure he was trying to accommodate his extra guests. If there was one thing I had learned about Elias, he was generous.

I hung out with three generations of Cole women while they went from store to store checking out everything Aspen had to offer. I browsed around and picked up a few things too. Besides the one package I left under the tree for Elias, I had nothing else for him. How in love could we be if we didn't exchange gifts? I could wrap the lavender bath salts and put them under the tree for me. That way Elias didn't appear inattentive. I'd just have to ask him where they were.

When we entered Doodles, I separated from the group and went in search of a holiday cookbook. I was debating between two when Gretchen snuck up on me.

"What are we having for dinner? Maybe I could help." Damn it. Caught with my hand in the jar.

"No, I just thought I'd try a new recipe or two. You know how much your brother likes to eat. He would probably enjoy something special." I wish I knew what she was thinking, but her face was a blank slate. The girl would be unbeatable in poker.

"You two are darling together. I've never seen my brother so attached. Well, not since . . ." She turned away and exhaled. "Do you know about Kimberly? It's not my place to bring it up, but I haven't seen him this happy since then."

"Don't worry, I know she broke his heart. I promise not to do the same. Your brother and I are—"

"Perfect for each other," she said, finishing my sentence. I was going to say friends first, and that would never change, but she was convinced she was right and wasn't the objective to fool them all? "That's why we're all here. To see for ourselves. We've been worried about him. He's too kind and soft-hearted to be alone. We thought he was damaged beyond repair and then you came along and patched his heart." She pulled the two books and me against her bosom and hugged me. "I'm glad you're here, Cici. I've always wanted a sister."

Oh shit, shit, shit. This was going too far, too fast. I had to put the brakes on right away. "Gretchen, Elias and I are at the beginning of our relationship. I wouldn't be marking your calendar for our wedding just yet."

"Got it." She giggled and then winked at me. What the hell? Who winks these days? I felt like we just exchanged some girl code I wasn't familiar with.

At the register, I purchased the two cookbooks and a book on fly-fishing I thought Elias might enjoy. Next, we moved to Spindles. The natural wool store sold hand-knitted goods, including sweaters and scarves. I was drawn to a blue scarf the exact color of Elias's sapphire eyes. Despite being cashmere, and way out of my budget, I purchased it. I could afford a small splurge with the amount he was paying me.

We ended the afternoon at the organic grocers, a place I insisted we stop to get eggnog, oranges, and cloves. There was no reason we couldn't imbibe while we made pomanders for the tree. Christmas was not about the presents. Sure, they were nice, but it was a time to enjoy the ones you loved, or in my case, to enjoy the ones Elias loved.

With our arms full, we went in search of the man himself. We found him walking out of the bookstore, his arms overwhelmed with packages. I'd never seen exuberance on him before, but that was the only way to describe the delighted smile gracing his face. The warmth of had entered his heart. He was embracing the season.

CHAPTER 8

Elias's dad and Uncle Fritz were asleep in the La-Z-Boy recliners downstairs. They had to have been up at the crack of dawn in order to arrive here so early this morning. Maggie covered them with throws before she headed upstairs with Izzy and Gretchen to take a nap. That left Elias and me on our own.

"They'll be hungry when they get up," I said as I walked into the kitchen. "What would you suggest I prepare for dinner?" I stood befuddled in front of the refrigerator. I was far from a chef, but I was confident I could whip up something edible.

"I'll take care of it. How about we order pizza? We can sit in front of the television and watch Christmas movies. I picked up a few today just for you." He shut the refrigerator and pulled me against him. I wanted to separate myself, but I was a magnet, and he was apparently my metal. Our simple attraction was too much to fight. I leaned into him and rested my cheek on his chest. There was no one to watch us, this wasn't part of the act.

"Mr. Scrooge picked up movies. Unbelievable." I reluctantly pulled away from his chest. "What did you get?"

Like a kid with a good report card he took my hand and pulled me toward the great room to show off what he'd bought. He rummaged through his bags and pulled out several DVDs. *Home Alone, A Christmas Carol, Miracle on 34th Street, It's a Wonderful Life,* and *A Christmas Story.*

"You got my favorites." I was beyond excited. What thrilled me more was looking across at Elias and seeing his gorgeous face beaming. *Oh, that smile was lethal.* Gretchen was right. He was so generous. I wished I could bottle his goodness and his smile so I could feel and see them when this was over. I reached my arms around him and held him close. "Thank you, Elias."

Again, I felt his lips in my hair, and it took so much strength to not tilt my head up and taste his lips again. "You're welcome, Chloe Lou Who."

Don't look up, Cici. Don't. Look. Up.

Elias retreated into his office to wrap presents. I snuck upstairs to do the same.

I sat on the bed—Elias's bed—and wrapped the gifts I'd bought him. I hoped he would like them. If I could accomplish one thing this holiday, it would be to help him have a wonderful week with his family.

Elias moved like a ghost through the house. He showed up without a sound and each time he snuck up behind me, I swear a year of my life had been taken. This time was no different.

With my back to the door, I sat Indian style on the bed, putting the finishing touches on his wrapped scarf. I was imagining it wrapped around his neck. His blue eyes were fighting against the cashmere for attention. Of course, his eyes would win.

When his hands touched my sides, I rose from the bed by inches. He tickled me from my hips to my armpits, and I couldn't control my laughter. He wouldn't let up. Within minutes I was pinned under him. He had straddled my body and pressed me between his thighs into the soft mattress. There was no way to get free even if I had wanted to, so I stopped fighting and he stopped tickling. I lay on the bed and looked up at a man who had turned into a boy. A happy boy.

When he leaned down, I closed my eyes and waited for his lips to touch mine, but they didn't. When I opened them again, he had the gift I'd just wrapped in his hands. *Was I relieved or disappointed?* Part of me wanted him to throw caution into the air and kiss me. The other part of me knew another kiss from him would change everything.

"For me?" He straightened his back and furrowed his brows in question.

"Yes, it's for you."

"Why?" He turned the package in his hand as if grading the wrapping job.

"Because it was perfect for you."

Putting the gift aside, his gaze as he looked at me, could only be called smoldering. "I'm beginning to think you're perfect for me." His head descended, and his mouth covered mine; all thought was lost. The kiss started soft as his tongue drifted across my own, tasting and teasing with care. The kiss quickly grew like a firestorm and became fierce and demanding as he explored my mouth and invaded my mind.

And there we were, locked in a passionate kiss when his mother walked into the room. Like teenagers caught with our pants down, we jumped from the bed and straightened our clothes.

Most people would have been embarrassed to walk in on such an intimate moment, but his mother looked pleased. Pleased with herself or pleased with us. I had no idea.

"I knocked, you didn't answer."

"Mom, we'll be downstairs in a few minutes. I was helping Cici with something."

"She seems to be breathing again. No additional mouth-to-mouth necessary. What a shame." She turned and walked out the door. I could hear her laugh all the way down the hallway.

"Cici, I'm sorry. You make me lose myself around you. Something about you is addictive. Your happiness is contagious, and I want it around me always."

"Elias, this is such a bad idea. I promised myself I'd never sleep with the boss again. You're the boss." I couldn't begin to describe the look he gave me. I couldn't tell if he was angry or hurt, but if I were going to protect myself I had to draw the line. And it was going to be right here on Elias's plush carpet.

"We aren't sleeping together, Cici. It was just a kiss." He sounded like I did this morning when I said something similar. When I dismissed the kiss, it was in an attempt to convince myself it was nothing. I'd been lying. Was he doing the same? That wasn't *just a kiss*. The man was lethal if he thought *that* was just a kiss.

To bring order back into our lives, I loaded his arms with wrapped gifts and asked him to take them downstairs. When he got to the door, he turned to look at me. Stopped. Stared. Then turned and walked away without a word. *What did that look mean?*

In the bathroom, I splashed cold water on my face and looked at myself in the mirror. My lips were kiss swollen and my cheeks reddened by passion . . . or maybe it was embarrassment. It had been years since a parent had caught me sneaking a kiss. With a twist, I piled my hair on top of my head and clipped it in place. While the Coles watched Christmas movies, I'd whip together something for tomorrow's breakfast. I was good at breakfast.

The entire gang was awake when I came downstairs. Elias was on the phone, ordering pizza. I slid past the family and into the kitchen. I could make a killer breakfast casserole. This was where my chef skills would sparkle. I hoped we had lots of eggs and cheese. When I opened the refrigerator I took a thorough look and found everything I needed and some things I didn't. Sitting on the second shelf was a cow's ass. I was certain of it. There was no place else a piece of meat that size could come from.

"Do you need help?" Gretchen took a seat across from where I was cutting green peppers and onions.

"No, I've got this. I'm just getting it ready for tomorrow morning. It will be the perfect breakfast before you all go skiing."

She set her book on the table and gave me a perplexed look. "You're going skiing too, right?"

"No, I'm not a good skier. I would only slow you down."

Elias ghosted into the kitchen. "She's going skiing. I hired an instructor for her. He'll work with her in the morning, and we'll all take a run in the afternoon." He grabbed a six-pack of soda from the refrigerator and left as fast as he'd entered.

"He's gotten bossy in his old age." Gretchen flipped through the pages of her book.

"Tell me about that book. It seems to be in the hands of every single girl on earth." After breaking twelve eggs, I began to whip them gently before adding the vegetables.

"It's simple. Basically, it says it takes twenty dates to fall in love. Forty hours really. The author claims that after twenty, two-hour dates, a person can tell if they've met their match or not. If after forty hours there are questions about the person's character, integrity, or things of that nature, then you should walk away. If the forty hours worked for you, then you're probably good to sign on for full-time."

"It's a good premise, but I'm sure it's not that easy." I poured a little cream in my eggs and continued to stir.

"I don't know. You and my brother look in love. How many dates have you been on?" She laid her hand on the book like it was the Bible.

This would have been the perfect time to confess my sins and tell her that her brother and I weren't in love, but I couldn't betray Elias. This whole ruse was important to him. He wanted a holiday free of badgering, and I would give that to him.

"I don't know. Lately, we seemed to be spending all our hours together. Does that count?"

"The author says forty hours. Would it matter how they were divided up? I would think spending long strings of time together would give you better insight. It shows how a person acts all day not just for two hours. Anyone can behave for two hours."

"What about you? Who are you spending your time with?" Her face flushed red. She tried to hide it, but I had her trapped with a *tell-me-everything* look.

"I've been seeing a guy named Dave Sparks for a couple weeks now. He's all right. I don't know if he's the one though. We kind of want different things. Family is important to me, and I want one. I'm twenty-seven, so I need to think about these things. He's thirty-five and has been married before. He has a kid and doesn't want any more."

"It sounds to me like you might have come up with a stumbling block. How many dates have you been on?" It would be interesting to see how this plays out, according to the book.

"I've got twenty hours invested. Which is half the time it would take to make a decision, and yet saying it out loud makes it all clear. We want different things. The problem is, he's so good in bed. That's hard to find these days." A blush, the color of a Gala apple, covered her skin. She really was like Elias with different parts. They were both so open, but their skin betrayed their verbal bravado.

"Sex is an important consideration. Although my mother once told me, you can correct bad in bed, you can't correct cheap." Saying it out loud was even funnier. She'd been mad at my dad for not getting her the purse she'd wanted. He'd bought the knock-off. In the end, she went back and bought the authentic brand, and he never noticed.

"How is Elias in bed? Does he need fixing? I don't want

details, but he has always been a guy that wants to please so . . ."

"Gretchen, I'm not talking penis size or sexual prowess with you." Of course, Elias would have perfect timing and walk in just as the word penis exited my mouth. The look on his face was priceless.

"What am I missing in here? And they say men are awful. I leave you girls for a few minutes, and you're talking about men's penises."

Hoping to make Elias's blush match his sister's, I walked over to him and slid my hand up his chest. "We weren't talking about just any penis, we were talking about yours." He looked at his sister and pointed toward the door.

"Out. Cici is in big trouble. Unless you want to be witness to me throwing her over my knee, you should leave now. The pizza is in the living room waiting." When his sister sat looking at us, he took a predatory lunge toward her that sent her running and squealing from the kitchen.

He was laughing when he took me by the arm. "We weren't talking about yours. I mean, your sister asked if you were good in bed, and I couldn't tell her, so I just made a funny. I promise I wasn't attacking your manhood."

"I'm not upset. I think it's funny. The funniest part is I have a feeling you'd like to know the answer to that question."

He let go of my arm, and I turned away so he couldn't see my face. I *did* want to know. I had a lot of questions that begged for answers, but I played stupid.

"What question is that?" I pulled the plastic wrap over

the sides of the pan. Breakfast was ready to throw in the oven tomorrow morning. The oven wasn't on, but it was getting hot in the kitchen.

"Whether I'm good in bed."

"You shouldn't eavesdrop."

"You shouldn't say things that could be misconstrued."

"You shouldn't stand there and be so tempting." I brushed past him and walked into the great room where his family was dishing up pizza. I looked at the boxes to find the one with the least meat on it. I was hoping I could pick it off inconspicuously. I was the only omnivore in a land of carnivores.

Elias rushed in after me and pulled a few pieces from a box. "This is for you." He handed me two slices full of artichokes and mushrooms. In that moment I knew I was a goner. He was too damned sweet, too damned considerate, and too damned sexy. *I* was too damned stupid to turn and run.

The sweet smile he gave me when I said thank you further melted my heart. So. Not. Fair.

I sat on the floor in front of the tree and nibbled on my pizza while I studied the Coles. Clint and Maggie sat on the couch and talked skiing. Fritz stood by the pizza boxes like a warrior guarding their contents. Gretchen leaned against her brother, who was leaning against the fireplace mantel. Izzy sat in the leather recliner watching me. What questions bounced around in her brain? She looked happy. In fact, they all looked happy, and that made me happy. Wasn't that what Elias wanted?

Each time I looked up, Elias was looking at me. There was warmth and appreciation in his eyes. Maybe even a little heat. Damn him for being so sexy. It was a constant challenge to keep my head in the real game. My mind and body were beginning to believe the lie.

His sister watched us both, her eyes held questions. Could Elias and I fool them all?

After we ate, we moved into the family room, which could only be described as the coolest man-cave ever. It was where we'd wrapped presents the night before. Had it only been a day? It felt like a lifetime ago. I needed a drink to calm my nerves and libido. Each time Elias looked at me, my internal furnace cranked up and threw another log on the fire.

When I returned from the bar area, all seats had been occupied leaving only the floor for me. I sat in front of Elias. It seemed the smart place to go, considering we were a "couple." It would have appeared odd for me to sit across the room. Another poor decision.

I wasn't on the floor for more than two minutes when he reached down and pulled me up on his lap. The muscles on this man. How I'd love for him to pick me up and carry me to bed. Hovering over my naked body, his arms would flex . . . *Cici! Head in the game.* He twisted me around so my legs hung over the side of the chair, and my cheek found the perfect place to rest against his chest.

"Comfortable?" His whisper floated over me like a heating blanket on high.

"Very." I sipped my wine and glanced at the screen. *Miracle on 34th Street* was starting, and I knew I wouldn't hear a single line of the movie. All I could hear was the rhythm of Elias's heart, and all I could feel was mine trying to keep pace.

"Let's go." He lifted me in his arms like I weighed nothing. I startled, remembering I'd had a glass in my hand. "You're fine. I've got you. You fell asleep."

I opened my eyes to see his family looking at us. His mom could light up an entire room with the wattage of her smile.

"I can walk." I struggled in his arms until he pulled me tight into his chest. He wasn't relenting. I was getting the full girlfriend treatment. I looked over his shoulder and waved goodnight to everyone in the room.

When we got to the room, he set me gently on my feet. "You can use the bathroom first. I'll get my bed ready while you're in there." He turned and walked into the closet.

I felt bad about making him sleep on the floor. So bad that I couldn't allow him to do it. Surely we could sleep in the same bed in our flannel pajamas and behave. Couldn't we?

"Elias, we can both sleep in your bed. It's certainly big enough to get lost in, and if you're worried about me molesting you in the middle of the night, we can put pillows in the middle as a barrier." The man came out of the closet wearing his flannel pajama bottoms, an Aerosmith T-shirt, and a smile. The slow, sweet, melting-panties smile.

We stood at the double sinks and brushed our teeth. I debated washing off my makeup. Even though he had seen me this morning, I wasn't sure if I wanted him to really *see* me. Our encounter this morning had been brief, and I had hidden behind the blanket. Did I really want to scar him for life?

Mom said every day you don't wash your face you age seven days. Not wanting to look a day over thirty, I took heed of her wisdom and scrubbed off the day's makeup.

He was lying in bed when I approached. My side of the bed had been turned back like a fine hotel. Rolled up like a log and placed in the center of the bed was a comforter. Disappointment crushed me. It would appear Elias questioned my self-control, or maybe . . . he questioned his own. We were walking a thin line between acting and actively flirting, and it was getting blurry. It all felt too real.

"Don't trust me?"

"I trust you, I just wanted to make you feel more comfortable. It was your suggestion."

I wanted to kick myself for saying anything, and yet the rolled up comforter was a defined line. A solid reminder this wasn't real. It was a job. Employer. Employee. Nothing more.

When I climbed into the soft sheets and turned to my side, the only thing I could see was the tube of fluffy down. It was a sad substitution for what, or rather who, I preferred to look at. Trying to be sneaky, I crushed down the comforter to get a final glimpse of him and came face to face with the man I knew would fill my dreams tonight.

The light behind him gave him an ethereal glow. We didn't say a word, just stared at each other for minutes on end. My mind was full of questions. How could Becca leave this man? How could Kimberly have broken his heart all those years ago? *How* could I stay on my side of the mattress all night long? That was the most difficult to answer.

"Thanks for everything, Cici. You're the most amazing woman."

"I'm not so special, Elias." I pulled blankets over my shoulder and snuggled deep into them.

"I disagree." He shifted his body and rolled over the barrier to kiss me on the forehead. When he turned back, the light went off, and we were cloaked in darkness.

Heat surrounded me. Not suffocating heat, but the kind of heat that made you want to stay in bed all day. It wasn't until my pillow moved I realized I wasn't on my side of the bed. Somehow I'd crept over and made myself comfortable on Elias's broad chest. His arm was wrapped around me and rested comfortably on my hip. His fingers splayed wide. All he needed to do was close his palm to get a handful of my ass.

Could I slip out from under him without waking him up? I had to try. When I picked his hand up from my hip, he pulled me in closer.

"Don't go anywhere. I'm too comfortable for you to move. Don't. Move." His voice was not the voice of a man who'd just woken up. I'd bet he'd been awake for a while.

I was mortified. "Oh my God. I'm sorry, Elias. Even though you put up a barrier I couldn't be trusted." I squirmed, trying to get loose of his grip, but he wouldn't let go. He laughed.

"I'm not complaining. Best night of sleep I've had in a

long time. You're a snuggler. There's no shame in that. You drifted over early into the night." His fingers brushed over the small of my back sending chills through my body. "I thought you were cold, so I loaned you my heat."

"I'm embarrassed."

"If that embarrasses you, I suppose I shouldn't tell you what you did with your hands." He held me tighter as I tried to get away.

"What? What did I do?" I groaned in shame. I couldn't be held responsible for what my body did while I slept. This was bad.

"Well, your hand slowly traced down my chest and slipped—"

"Oh my God, don't tell me. I'm so sorry." He rolled over so we were looking eye to eye. His eyes flashed with mischief.

"Your hand slowly traced down my chest and slipped off just before you jerked it back and smacked me in the nose." The bed shook with his laughter.

"You're awful." In spite of his grip on me, I managed to get into a seated position next to him. "You had me thinking I had . . . Anyway, you're despicable." This time I straddled him. I was hardly large enough to pin him down, but he didn't fight me. In fact, he raised his hands and put them high on my thighs. The heat he stirred warmed me from the inside out.

Damn him for looking so alluring. Damn his sexy morning hair and the scruff that screamed to be touched. Damn his broad shoulders that led to narrow hips. The same hips my thighs were squeezing right now. *Arghhh. Focus.*

"I would have enjoyed your hand if it had . . ." Oh, the

man didn't need kisses to melt panties. If I sat across his body any longer, I'd be stripping mine off and begging him to take me.

I pulled his hands off my thighs and held mine in front of him. "The only thing these hands will be doing is turning on the shower. Can you go downstairs and preheat the oven to 350 degrees? I need to get that casserole in if we are going to eat before we ski."

"I'd rather stay here with you." He pulled his lush lower lip forward in a pout that could thaw ice, but I couldn't go there.

"Not an option, slick." *That's right, hold steady. You got this.*

"Too bad."

Was that genuine disappointment I heard?

I climbed off his body—missing his heat immediately —and couldn't help but notice the rise in his flannels. Not to embarrass him or myself, I turned toward the bathroom and didn't look back. I wanted to look back, but I didn't have the courage. Looking back would have required follow through, and I couldn't. Wouldn't.

When I stepped out of the shower, there was a cup of Earl Grey on the counter. I immediately looked at the shower and wondered how much he could have seen. Absolutely nothing but a shadow. The rain glass was nearly opaque. I sipped the tea and sighed. This was going to be some lucky girl's life. Right now I was the lucky girl in the beta run. I could get used to his warm body curled around me, and hot tea waiting on the counter after my showers.

Wrapped in a towel, I entered the empty bedroom. If I hurried, I could probably get dressed before he returned.

No such luck. He must have a beacon for inopportune times. The door closed just as I was tugging my ski pants out of my bag.

"Casserole is in the oven. It went in five minutes ago." He came to stop beside me. I could see something in his eyes. Something childlike and playful.

I had no idea how I knew, but somehow I did. He planned to swipe my towel and leave me standing naked in the center of his room. Well, if the man wanted to see me naked, how could I deny him? He'd brought me tea and that deserved a reward. I dropped the towel. He dropped his jaw.

"Fuck. Me," he groaned.

"Pick your lips up off the floor and go shower." I pulled on my underwear and bra while he watched in a trance. "Make it a cold one." It was like the man had never seen boobs before. Well, he'd never seen mine.

"You're in trouble. You're not playing fair. You tell me we can't investigate this thing between us because I'm the boss, and then you parade the goods in front of me. You're cruel, heartless I'd say." He had the look of a father chastising his child. "Maybe I should fire you, then there wouldn't be a boss problem." He turned around and walked into the bathroom, taking my confidence with him.

What had I been thinking? He was right. I crawled into his body all night, and then I stripped myself bare to punish him for teasing me. In reality, I was punishing myself because I knew if I said the word, it would be a go and not a no with him. And I knew it would be wonderful. That was why I couldn't let it go anywhere. I didn't want to lose a piece of my heart. If I made love to this man, I'd never get that part of me back. *Why?*

It had been six days since I'd met Elias Cole, and if my count was right, I'd spent over fifty hours in his presence, not counting the time spent in his bed. *Twenty Dates to Love* might have got it right. Forty hours and I was falling hard for my boss.

It wasn't a matter of why I was falling hard. It was simply a matter of *how could I not?* I'd always wanted someone attentive to my needs, kind and generous, someone with a wonderful sense of humor, and someone who loves family. Add in Elias is drop-dead sexy, cute, and delicious, and he was the perfect combination. *How could I not fall for him?* Shit.

When everyone gathered for breakfast, I had the island set up with food and the dining room with plates and silverware. I poured coffee and juice while the Coles got their meals and took their seats. Elias entered dressed in body-fitting ski pants and thanked me for breakfast as he brushed his lips across mine. Before he could separate from me, I pulled his lip into my mouth and sucked it gently.

I'd given him and us a lot of thought this morning. Yes, Elias was my boss, but I knew where I stood with him. This wasn't a relationship. Elias was simply offering me the moment, and why shouldn't I take it? I was thirty years old and capable of a fling.

"Don't start something you can't finish, Cici," he warned. "You left me hard and in need of a cold shower." He whispered the words in my ear. "Don't you feel bad?" The brush of heated air sailed over my skin and made me tingle all the way from my hardened nipples to my heated sex.

"I do, and I promise to make it up to you later." I left him standing, surprised, by the eggs.

When we got to the resort, everyone was excited to ski except Grandma Izzy and Uncle Fritz; they planned to camp out in the lodge and drink cocoa in front of the fireplace. The others were looking forward to hitting the slopes as soon as possible.

Grateful to have an instructor, I was excited to have some guidance. The last thing I needed was to be laid up in a body cast for months.

Suited up and equipped, we all piled into the seven-seater Clint had rented and headed to the slopes. I was to meet my instructor at the green run under the ski school sign. The Coles were heading straight for the double black diamond. Elias kissed me dizzy before he left with a promise to meet for lunch.

While I waited, I thought about how wonderful the Coles were. Grandma Izzy was a bit of a pistol. The woman had absolutely no filter. As we were cleaning up the pizza last night she'd asked if my boobs were real. I dished her back some of her own by telling her that boobs as nice as mine couldn't be bought.

"Hey, are you Cici?" A white-haired man glided to a stop beside me. I had expected a young Scandinavian guy named something like Lars, not a younger skinnier version of Santa Claus.

"Yep, and you are?" I leaned on my poles waiting for instruction.

"Late, sorry. I'm Dave. Let's hop on this run, so I can see what I'm working with." And we did. Again and again and again. After Dave was confident I was getting the whole paralleling thing down, I graduated to a blue run. By eleven o'clock I was up to red. I had managed to stay on my feet for at least fifty percent of the runs, too. And being with an instructor had its perks, like a front-of-the-line pass.

The air felt good on my face as I swooped down the hill. Elias was right. A bit of instruction could go a long way. Until an out-of-control skier took me out at the knees, I was feeling confident. How come it's never the skiing that kills you but the other skiers?

I'm not sure how I tumbled the rest of the way down the hill with my skis on. Maybe because I was tangled up with the kamikaze skier. However, when I stopped, *every-thing* hurt.

Dave was leaning over me with concern in his eyes. "Don't move, Cici. I've called Ski Patrol to come and get you."

Ski Patrol? Surely I didn't need Ski Patrol. All I needed was a helping hand to get up. My ass was almost numb from the snowpack below me. "I'm good. What about the other guy?" I looked around and saw him lying next to me. His right leg was not in a position natural to the human body.

All I could hear was a woman yelling at him, saying she knew he wasn't ready for the run, and he should have listened to her. He was probably trying to get away from her. I knew if someone were squawking at me like that, I would have raced away to my death as well.

Next thing I knew, Elias was by my side, his eyes filled with concern, the muscles of his jaw rigid, and his lips pulled thin. I could feel the tension emanating from him. Maybe I was really hurt. My body ached, but nothing actually hurt. I wiggled my toes in my boots. They seemed fine. Cold, but fine. I wiggled my fingers, and those were okay as well. His hands searched my body for injuries. Maybe I should pretend to be hurt then he could check me out again.

"I'm okay, just help me up. My butt is cold." Elias's eyes softened. He put his hand behind my back and helped me into a sitting position. Nope, nothing broken. "It appears I bounce pretty well."

"God, Cici, he took you out at the knees." His words were hurried and emotional. "I was waiting at the bottom of the hill." He released the bindings, which took the pressure off my knees. "It was time for lunch and I thought I'd surprise you. Instead, you surprised me." When his hands came up under my armpits and lifted me, I felt as light as air. This man could toss my five-feet-five-inch body around like it weighed nothing.

On two feet again, I shook out the kinks. My neck would be a bit sore and tomorrow my back would ache like a seventy-year-old with rheumatism, but I was in one piece. Ski Patrol put speed-racer into the sled and took him away. He didn't fare well in our collision.

"Really, Elias, I'm made of tough stuff. I'm good. I'll be a little sore, but maybe my boss will let me drink on the job and sleep in a little tomorrow."

"I hear he's pretty flexible." His lips were on mine for

an instant. Not nearly enough time. "I also hear he serves tea in bed." All I really heard of that was *bed.* He dipped back to my lips, and we stood in the middle of the run kissing until our faces were wind-burned and our lips chapped. Every part of my body was thawing under his heavenly kisses. And his hands, cupping my face and rubbing gentle circles on my cheeks . . . It was when a passing skier told us to get a room we parted.

"Where's Dave?" My instructor had disappeared with my skis.

"I dismissed him. He'll see you tomorrow if you want to ski after we open presents."

Was it really Christmas Eve already?

With the thawing of my body came the roaring from my stomach. I was starving. Skiing took a lot out of you. "Are you going to feed me, or do I need to find another ski bum to snuggle with in order to get food?"

"There will be no mystery ski bum volunteering to feed you or keep you warm. That's my job." He sounded so possessive, and he looked the same. His eyes claimed what his lips could not.

"You're hired as my official ski bum."

"Good, now we can get past the boss thing. You've got me needing you. Bad."

Shocked at his declaration, I gave him a soft punch in the arm. "Let's go before I freeze to death." I was beginning to realize I needed him just as badly.

We walked down the slope hand in hand. Elias used his skis as a walking stick. *Stick, step.* Stick, step until we reached the bottom. Our boots *ka-clunked* all the way into the lodge where we joined his family at a table set for lunch. Elias had thought of everything.

"We were beginning to think you guys ditched us and went home," Gretchen said.

"No, there was an accident on the slope." Elias looked at me again, making sure I was in one piece.

"They brought a man down on a stretcher. I wonder what he'd hit," Uncle Fritz said.

I raised my hand slowly. "Me." I knew exactly where Elias got his dropped-jaw look. It was plastered on every face around the table.

"And you're alive to tell about it? Oh my goodness, Cici. Are you okay?" Maggie was out of her chair and at my side immediately. Like her son, she felt me up and down. Not the same experience, but it was heartwarming she cared. I was going to hate when this was over because I really liked his mother.

"I'm fine. I'll be sore tomorrow, but today I'm feeling good, and I'll feel better once I get an Irish coffee in me." Elias took the hint and called the waitress over. Irish coffees were ordered for the whole table.

Izzy broke into the conversation with her personal flair. "In my day I would have sent everyone off skiing and stayed in bed if you know what I mean." She gave us a wink-wink.

Laughing, Elias said, "Cici tried to tempt me, but I said nope, my family is here." He stopped laughing when I kicked his shin under the table. One good whack above his boot was all it took. Let the games begin.

"You're such a liar." When it came out, I realized I made it sound like we had done the deed. Elias appeared to take great joy as I tumbled over my tongue. Thankfully the lunch Maggie had ordered arrived, along with the round of Irish coffees. Nothing healed frayed nerves and muscle aches like Irish whiskey.

After lunch, it was decided I'd take Grandma and Uncle Fritz home while the others took the black double diamond and skied down the bowl to the house. I was happy to stand in as chauffeur. My body was beginning to feel the effects of the bounce down the hill, and a soak in a hot bath was calling me.

When we entered the house, Izzy and Fritz headed upstairs to their rooms. I followed suit and made it as far as the bed. I crawled under the covers and inhaled the scent of Elias. It brought back the memory of his kisses on the slope. When I fell asleep, there were no sugarplum fairies in my head, but my mind was filled with visions of Elias. Naked.

CHAPTER 10

The mattress dipped, and I pried my eyes open from a sound sleep. Elias was sitting on the edge of the bed with a glass of wine and a soft look. He brushed his fingers through my hair and ran his thumb across my lips. I could get used to waking up to him.

"I ran you a bath." He rubbed my back, and I winced; those muscles would never forgive me for the abuse I'd given them today. "Grandma said you had come up to take one and feared you had drowned. Since I found you asleep and still in your ski clothes, I figured you'd never made it there." He set the wineglass on the nightstand and began to undress me.

I pulled his hand from the front zipper of my ski bibs. "I got it. Go visit your family." *Why was I shy now?*

"Stop. This morning you flashed me, so you don't have anything I haven't seen. I'm just going to get you undressed so you can take advantage of the bath I ran for you." The man was definitely looking out for me. "I even put your lavender salts in it. As for my family, they all went to take a nap. I'm sure they'll be out until dinner, which will be Chinese takeout. No need for anyone to cook."

It was a relief I wouldn't have to cook. I hadn't come to terms with the meat thing yet. I'd gotten away with no one noticing my eating habits thus far. At lunch, I'd nibbled on the salad and ate a few potato wedges. I didn't care if they knew I was a vegetarian, but I didn't want them to know I'd never cooked a prime rib. It was going to be a challenge, but they didn't need to know how inept I really was. I'd read those damn cookbooks tonight, so I could cook the hell out of that bovine ass tomorrow.

When I tried to move, I wasn't capable. My arms and legs felt like jelly as they flopped against the mattress. I was definitely going to need his assistance.

He slipped the zipper down slowly. This wasn't a sexy assisted striptease but more of a painful discarding of excess fabric. I managed to sit and then stand in order to get my gear off. First to go were the ski bibs, then the thermal underwear. I was left standing in my panties and bra. Not the sexy ones I saved for dates, but the utilitarian ones I wore to the doctor. Plain white. No frills. Not sexy.

I trudged toward the bathroom with legs that felt weighed down with cinder blocks. Who would have thought tumbling down an intermediate slope could feel like getting hit by a truck? An eighteen-wheeler. Fully loaded.

"The bath should help with your sore muscles. The lavender will help you relax. The wine is just for fun."

"I like fun," I said as I glanced around and saw the effort he'd put into the bath.

The flicker of candlelight danced off shimmering

bubbles. A glass of dark red wine sat on the ledge of the massive tub. A tub built for two. Elias was behind me, guiding me toward my therapy.

"There are lots of bottles of fun downstairs. I'll let you get in the bath, and I'll check on you in a few minutes." The moment he left, I stripped off the coyote-ugly undergarments and slid into the hot water. It flowed over my body like a magic elixir. Everywhere it touched, my body sang with relief.

Bubbles settled over the top of the water covering everything but my head. I closed my eyes and sank deep into the water. The heat enveloped me, and I was lost in luxury.

The scent of cloves and citrus fought against the lavender. My heavy lids peeled back slowly. Elias sat on the edge of the tub and smiled a trillion-dollar smile. The neck of a cabernet bottle swung between two fingers.

"You're behind on the fun. Drink up." He topped off my glass. Smooth and fruity, it went down quick and easy. Beads of sweat dripped down my forehead. When I tried to swipe at them, I ended up with a face full of bubbles. Elias reached over and brushed off the froth.

My heart tumbled into the deep end of the tub and drowned in lust. Here was this man who had hired me to decorate his house for his family. Who had hired me to be his girlfriend for his family. Who was treating me like *I was* family. If only. I fell a little bit in love, but I was a lot in lust. Add the wine, and that was a recipe for a lot of fun. *Oh, fuck it.*

Catching him off guard, I yanked his arm and pulled him into the tub. I'd been told you only lived once, and I decided to live now.

He plunged into the bath fully clothed. With his hand raised high above his head, he saved the expensive cabernet from getting diluted by bath water. Water sloshed over the side and onto the floor.

He pulled the bottle to his lips and drank. "I prefer to be naked when I bathe." His feet were still in the air when he kicked his shoes to the ground and curled himself into the tub, socks and all.

I obviously didn't think this through. I was naked, and he was clothed. I had a dry glass, and he had a full bottle. I wanted everything he had to offer. Out of the water, I rose, my muscles, although sore, were relaxed and flexible. On my knees, I sat in front of him and tried to even the playing field. His Adam's apple bobbed with each swallow. His face lit with wonder.

It was tough to drag his soggy polo shirt over his head, especially because he refused to let go of the wine, but I was committed. And by the heat in his eyes, he wasn't going to fight.

I ran my hands over his heated chest. My fingers explored the hills and valleys of his muscles. Pressing my breasts against him, I reveled in the feel of his hair against my sensitive nipples. They rose, seeking him—his touch.

The rugged sound of desire rumbled through him. I leaned back to see his face, and his expression was carnal. He wanted me as much as I wanted him. It showed in his heavy lids and the lips he'd just licked with his delectable tongue.

Next to go were his saturated socks. When I rose to position myself to remove his pants, he took advantage of my proximity and pulled a hardened nipple into his mouth. It was my turn to groan. He set my body on fire.

I yanked and pulled at his pants but they weren't budging. I would have cut them off if scissors had been handy, but sadly I was not equipped to cut my way to his treasure. Thankfully, he stood in front of me and dropped his khakis.

Wow, treasure was an understatement. I'd found the freaking hope diamond. Rock hard, and glistening in the glow of the candlelight.

"Are you sure?" He knelt in front of me, and I took pleasure in his desire for me. His arms snaked around my waist and over my backside, pulling me against his arousal. We moaned in unison. "What changed your mind? I thought there was no sleeping with the boss."

"It's Christmas, and I've been naughty. I imagine I deserve a bit of Cole." I ran my hand between us and gripped his hardness. It flexed in my palm. Heavy and engorged, it was ready. He was ready.

"You want Cole for Christmas? I'll give you a lot of Cole for Christmas." He maneuvered my body so I was prone in the tub. We'd splashed most of the water out when he'd tumbled in. There were mere inches left. Just enough to make us slick. Enough to make it fun.

"So you used condoms, IUD, and the pill?" I wanted to get the important stuff out of the way so we could get to the good stuff.

"Yes. You?" He reached for the pocket of his pants. The leather wallet he pulled from it was ruined, but he didn't seem to mind. He pulled out a foil packet and waved it in front of my face.

"Pill and condoms. He didn't want to risk pregnancy. It's up to you. I'm clean." He seemed shocked I'd allow him to go bareback, but I'd been cautious my whole life. I wanted to feel him, really feel him. *Only him.*

He tossed the packet aside and lowered himself against me. Our tongues battled, our breath hitched. We made love with our mouths, and when I clawed at his back, he buried himself deep inside me, stretching me, filling me.

"I've wanted this since you left a gingerbread man on the table for me to decorate." He began to move in a slow sensual slide. "Actually, I wanted you the minute you showed up at my house and began bossing me around, but I wasn't free to want." He was watching me, I was watching him, and nothing was more important than this very moment. "Now I am, and I find you irresistible."

As he moved inside me, something profound happened. I fell in love. In a week, he'd become a part of me as necessary as my blood and bones. And *that* terrified me.

How could I fall so hard and fast? He touched his lips to mine, pulled away, and growled, "This is so much more than you or I could have imagined."

He put words to my thoughts. *Yes, this was more.*

My body quivered from his motion, the pressure, the rhythm, but I flew over the edge at his words and he followed me. We lay spent, soaking wet in three inches of water mixed with cabernet. The bottle floated near my dripping wet curls. We would need another bottle of fun. This one had made the ultimate sacrifice.

He pressed his forehead to mine. "Wow." One word that ended with a kiss. When he released my mouth he continued to worship my body with soft kisses planted on my lips, eyes, cheeks, and neck. "You're an incredibly beautiful woman."

In awe of the man, I couldn't utter a word. He was everything. Everything and more.

When the water turned cold, he shifted. "I'll start the shower." He stepped from the tub, and I got the first look at his buns of steel. Globes of perfection waiting for my hands to explore the combination of soft skin and hard muscle. I rinsed the wine-infused water down the drain and stepped out to join him.

The shower sprayed from multiple jets. Steam rose and was trapped by the ceiling-high glass. We stood together in the fog, the thick atmosphere adding to the mystery of the moment. With gentleness, he cleansed my body and massaged my muscles. I was silly putty in his hands.

I explored every inch of his gloriousness under the ruse of washing him. I skimmed his broad shoulders and let my soapy hands find their way down his back. Slick fingers caressed and kneaded his firm ass. Kneeling, I rubbed his strong thighs and muscular calves. When I stood, I wrapped my arms around his waist, pressed my face against his prickly chest, and held on in fear I'd wake from this dream dressed in ski pants and ugly cotton underwear.

It seemed like words would ruin the moment and yet his were perfect. "Cici, I don't know how you ended up in my life, but you're working your way into my heart."

I nearly puddled at his feet. It was the perfect thing to say at the perfect moment. I didn't dare tell him I was falling as well. I'd learned not to verbalize my weakness. The last time I told a man I loved him, he told me that was sweet and then cheated on me. Love was a four-letter word that made people dash in the wrong direction. Speechless, I reached up and gently kissed him on his lips.

Grr . . . the rumble of my stomach echoed in the tile enclosure. We both looked down and knocked heads in the process. Laughter silenced my growling stomach.

He stepped out first and grabbed a towel from the cupboard. He didn't see to himself. Instead, he wrapped me up like a mummy and dried me off.

"I looked at the take-out menu, and they have an eggplant dish with vegetarian sauce. They also have a vegetarian egg drop soup." He had taken the time to investigate, and that meant so much. "What do you want me to order for you?"

My ex would have ordered what he wanted and told me to pick the meat out and eat the rest.

"It all sounds perfect. You order, and I'll be down in a minute." I had to reapply my makeup. What didn't get removed while my face dragged along the snowpack was now running down my cheeks after our steamy shower. *And yet he'd called me beautiful.*

I wrapped the towel around my body and attempted to pull myself together. I'd just experienced the most amazing sex with the most amazing man. My face was flush, and my body tingled with the excitement of finally finding someone worthy of my heart.

CHAPTER 11

I skimmed through the cookbook to make sure I didn't have to prepare anything tonight, and it was a good thing I did. The recipe called for lots of chopped herbs. That was something I could definitely get out of the way. The book said something about trimming off the excess fat and saving it. Yuk. Why feed these animals so much if you don't want them to have fat? Ew. The thought turned my stomach.

I'd put on a comfortable pair of jeans and a sweater my mom had knitted. We had a Christmas tradition in my family. Members had to don the ugliest Christmas sweater known to man, and my mom's claim to fame was creating them.

Even though I couldn't be with them, I'd wear this monstrosity of a sweater in honor of my family. It was a snowman riding a reindeer. It's head perfectly situated over one breast giving it the appearance of lopsided boobs. The best part was the wiggly eyes my mother glued to the reindeer. The black pupils moved with each step, drawing the eyes to my chest.

When I made it downstairs, I headed straight for the kitchen. Herbs, lots of herbs, needed chopping. Grandma Izzy was sitting at the counter when I pulled the rosemary, sage, thyme, and parsley from the refrigerator.

"You're glowing, Cici, in spite of that ugly sweater. That bath must have done you good." She smiled at me with a knowing smile. My reflection showed in the kitchen window, and I swore I was the color of purple cabbage.

"A hot bath and a glass of wine can change a life." It had certainly changed mine.

"Yes, so can a hot man and a king-sized bed." She picked up her glass and sipped. She studied me like a gemologist studies a diamond.

"Where is your hot man and king-sized bed?" I asked, hoping to redirect the attention. I didn't want to be having a birds and bees conversation at thirty with Elias's widowed grandmother. I liked her. However, I'd just made love to Elias for the first time, and I wanted that moment to be mine for a while longer.

She put her wine glass down and asked, "What kind of birth control do you use? I'm hoping the ineffective kind because I'm not getting any younger and need great-grandchildren before I die." She gave me an *I'm cute look* old people and children give when they know they've said something inappropriate.

"Sorry to bust your bubble, Ms. Izzy, but there will be no little Elias Coles running around anytime soon." Of course, *that* came out of my mouth the minute he walked in with his hands full of Chinese take-out bags.

"What's this about little Elias Coles?" He placed the bags on the counter, then leaned over and gave me a kiss. Not a deep one, but a genuine kiss on the lips with a tease of his tongue.

Was I supposed to say *your grandma wants to poke a hole in the condom we didn't use because she wants great grandbabies?* I didn't know what to say. As it turns out I didn't have to say anything.

"Elias, I'm seventy-four years old, and not getting any younger. I like this girl. She's perfect for you in every way." Izzy glanced my way. Her eyes landed on my middle. "Besides, she has child-bearing hips. I'm sure she can give me a few babies before I die."

I was speechless, as I'd never had anyone analyze my hips for birthing babies before. When I turned to Elias, he had turned a shade of crimson that matched the wine in his grannie's glass. "I'll have to give that some thought." He slid behind me and grabbed my hips. His fingers tightened on my hipbones dragging me back against him. "She does have perfect hips, Grandma, you are right about that." He buried his face in the crook of my neck and nibbled. "And she tastes as sweet as she is."

"Should I leave?" Izzy asked. She topped off her wine and began to unpack the food.

"Yes, Grandma, we are going to do it right here on the kitchen floor."

Izzy was obviously used to his smart mouth. "Pfft." She waved her hand in a dismissive fashion and continued to unpack the food. "Don't let me interrupt."

"Both of you need to stop. You're talking about me like a breeding mare. Elias, go help your grandmother. Izzy, you'd have more luck asking Santa for babies." I began to chop the herbs while the family filed into the kitchen to eat.

Elias leaned into me and whispered, "I'd like to be between those child-rearing hips about now." He kissed my cheek and walked off.

Funny how he had a way of voicing my thoughts.

Gretchen sidled up to me and pulled the rosemary from the stems. "Herbed prime rib? That sounds so good. What temperature do you cook yours at?"

I had no idea what to tell her. I hadn't read that far in the book. "Ummm, you know, hot enough to kill it." I tried to hide behind a giggle, but she didn't appear to buy it.

"You don't kill a prime rib, Cici, you merely scare it to medium rare." She pulled the knife from my hands and led me to the dinner table where everyone was seated.

I sat between Elias and Maggie. We passed the dishes to the right and everyone helped themselves. Plenty of dishes were Cici friendly. Steamed vegetables. Vegetarian egg drop soup. Eggplant in black bean sauce. Bok choy and shiitake mushroom stir-fry. There were also many carnivore dishes like crispy duck, beef with broccoli, chicken with cashews, and pork fried rice. There was enough food to feed the Coles for days. That could be a bonus. Less cooking for me.

Maggie tapped her glass and stood. "I want to make a toast to Cici for making my son happy again." She lowered her head and kissed me on the cheek. I felt terrible about our ruse. "And, Elias, please buy this girl some sweaters. That one is ghastly." All eyes went to my sweater.

"I'll have you know my mother knitted me this

sweater." I reached for my best hurt voice. Izzy had already called my sweater atrocious. I'd play this up and give them a bit of their own stuff back. They were sure good at dishing it out.

"Now, Maggie, that wasn't nice," Clint said. "Cici obviously likes her sweater." He looked at my sweater and shook his head. "Who are we to judge? Don't forget she's cooking our dinner tomorrow; you don't want to offend her." It was awful, but I had them.

"My mother knitted until her fingers blistered to make this sweater for me. Feel it, as far as fifty-fifty blends go, it's pretty soft." I put my arm in the center of the table and offered a feel to anyone who dared. No one did. They looked at me with pity. It was time to come clean, otherwise, they might lose their appetites. "I challenge you to find one as lovely. And next year you can join the ugly sweater contest, but I'll have you know the Craigs take their ugly sweater contest seriously."

Laughter erupted at the table. Even quiet Uncle Fritz was chuckling.

"I thought we were going to have to have an intervention," he said, right before he stuffed his mouth full of duck.

"I love that idea. I say we adopt Cici's family tradition and look for the most distasteful sweater we can find, but Cici is banned from wearing that twice." Elias talked like we would spend our next holiday together. It was part of the subterfuge for sure, but it did sound appealing. Despite being away from my family, I felt home. Part of a family. It felt like Christmas.

After dinner, I went back to herb chopping while

Gretchen cleaned up. Elias had gone to the living room to turn on Christmas music and set up some kind of surprise for everyone.

"Time to come clean." Gretchen leaned against the counter and crossed her arms.

"About what?" Holy shit. Did she know Elias and I weren't really an item? How was I going to get out of this?

"I've been here for two days, and you haven't eaten anything but vegetables, eggs, and cheese. I asked about cooking the prime rib and you said you were going to kill it. How do you plan to pull off cooking dinner when you don't eat meat?"

Shit. Shit. Shit. Gretchen is far more observant than her brother. I'd shared multiple meals with him, and he hadn't had a clue. "Oh, that. I didn't want you guys to worry about getting sick from E. coli, Salmonella, or Campylobacter jejuni."

"Campila what?"

I waved her off with a toss of my hand and said, "It's a food-borne bacteria that can make you sick. Eating animals can be dangerous."

"Yeah, especially if they're still alive." She began to laugh uncontrollably.

I waited for her to settle down. "Don't say anything, okay? In truth, I wanted your mother to like me and to shout out I'm a vegetarian could freeze her meat-eating heart. She may fear her son will starve to death being with me." I was so impressed with myself for coming up with that thought on the fly. And if the truth were told, I did want her to like me. Elias and I were developing something together. I wasn't sure if it would turn out to be anything, but I was hopeful because my heart was fully engaged.

"Your secret is safe with me."

"What secret is that?" Elias seemed to have some powerful magic that brought him into conversations at the most inopportune times.

"My famous herbed prime rib recipe."

"Oh, now it's famous?" He slid in behind me and pulled me against him. His hands wrapped around my waist and splayed across my stomach. It was such an intimate and knowing touch. The heat of his body felt so comforting. I needed his reassurance, knowing his sister was watching me the way a hawk watched a field mouse.

"Well, historical in any event." Turning around in his arms, I wrapped mine around his waist and squeezed. Burying my face in his chest, I sucked in the spicy scent of him.

"Hey, Gretchen, can you finish up in here? I need a few minutes alone with Julia Child." Again, Gretchen laughed. She was still laughing when Elias led me upstairs to his bedroom.

As soon as the door was closed he led me to the bed where he reached inside my pants and stroked my bottom. I moaned in response. His hands raced up my back and reached for my bra clasp. Oh, this man had dangerous, skillful hands, and I didn't want him to stop. It was like he had a thousand fingers, and they were touching me everywhere at once. His tongue danced with mine as if we'd kissed each other a million times. My skin was on fire. My panties were drenched. "What are you doing?" I whispered between kisses, praying he'd continue.

"I'm spending quality time with you." He pulled at my sweater, but I stopped his progress.

Panting, I said, "We can't do this right now. Your family is downstairs waiting for us." His hands stalled at the hem of my sweater. "Didn't you say something about a surprise?" His growl made my insides twist. It was sexy and sensual. The kind of growl a man released when he wanted what he couldn't have. Judging by the fierce hard-on pressed against me, he wanted me.

"I can't stop thinking about how much I love baths now." He wrapped one hand around my bottom and another around my head. His fingers laced through my curls. Our lips met in the center, his head rising, mine lowering, each of us seeking the other again. When his tongue probed for access, I sunk completely against him, giving up any control I had. It was minutes before I came up for air.

"I'm definitely a fan of baths." Somehow we had turned so we were both lying on our sides. "I'd never had a bath like that before, and I must say you massaged all the kinks from my body."

"I hope I didn't smooth all your kinkiness out. I was kind of looking forward to finding more tonight."

"Promise?"

"Absolutely."

"I'm excited."

"I'm impatient."

"You'll have to wait."

"Pure torture"

"For both of us."

"Are you ready to go downstairs?" I wasn't ready, but his family had come a long way to see him. I couldn't keep him all to myself, even though that was exactly what I wanted. "Oh, by the way, your sister is too observant. She knows."

"Knows what?" He lifted on his elbow, a look of concern on his face.

"That I'm a vegetarian." The look of relief completely erased his concern.

"So, that's the secret that's safe with her. You know, no one would think less of you if you came out of the vegetarian closet." He tucked a rogue curl behind my ear before he brushed his thumb over my kiss-swollen lips.

"You're losing track of the situation. We aren't pretending I'm not a vegetarian, we're pretending I'm your girlfriend, who just happened to be an excellent cook." Everything had become so muddy the last couple of days.

"I don't feel like I'm pretending anymore. This is real, Cici." He pulled me into his body, and it was a good thing because after hearing him say he didn't feel our relationship was pretend, I felt like I was flying. His firm embrace held me steady. Maybe getting Cole for Christmas was a good thing after all.

"It feels real. My heart wants it to be real, but I'm scared that after the holidays are over things will go back to normal. I'm okay if this is just a one-off kind of thing. Knowing what this is helps temper my attachment to you."

"I'm not going to be like your ex. I'm not using you for what you can bring me. I'm getting attached to you, Cici, and I'm not likely to let you go."

My heart bounced with happiness around my chest.

He wasn't going to let me go. "Maybe your family can fend for themselves for a while after all." My hands slipped inside his shirt to brush across his stone-hard stomach. He hissed the minute my fingers skimmed up and over his nipples. Slowly, he pulled my hands from his chest and brought my fingers to his mouth. His tongue grazed my knuckles, sending shivers straight to my sex.

"Actually, this surprise is more for you than it ever was for them." He pushed himself to a sitting position and looked at me like a dieter looks at a hot fudge sundae. He wanted to devour me, but I wasn't on the menu. *Yet.* Something told me he would have an immense appetite later. And knowing *that* allowed me to drag myself from the bed.

Once he was completely "ready", we walked hand in hand down the stairs. It must be hard being a man. Pun intended.

Gretchen sat at the Christmas tree, counting the packages like a little kid. Uncle Fritz and Clint were on the sofa reading. Maggie and Izzy were sitting in front of the window, eating truffles and looking at the bowl in front of them. I was so happy I'd added the extras his family was enjoying. My presence and contributions were valued.

The moon was just peeking over the mountain, its silver glow reflected off the white snow. It was almost Christmas.

"Everyone needs to go to the entertainment room or as Cici refers to it as 'the man cave.'" Elias herded his family like a well-trained border collie. On the bar in front of every seat was a gingerbread man. Bowls of candies and bags of icing were placed between each monster-sized cookie.

"Are we having a contest?"

"Yes. Cici loves Christmas more than anyone I know, but she also has a competitive streak in her. Note the ugly sweater. I thought we could decorate these things and vote on them." He had set this whole thing up for me. "Whoever wins gets to choose next year's Christmas location."

I can't remember a time when a man had shown me that kind of consideration. It was probably the most thoughtful gift anyone had ever given me. I turned and wrapped my arms around him. "This is going to be so much fun." My voice sang out about an octave higher than usual.

He pulled a barstool out for me and lifted me into it. "Let's have some holiday fun." His lips brushed lightly against mine. I wanted more. I wanted to grab his hand and race him to the bedroom. However, his family was taking their seats along the bar and everyone seemed ready to go.

Elias filled the air with Christmas music while we attacked the gingerbread men. Even Clint and Uncle Fritz gave it their best shot. Uncle Fritz seemed to get in touch with a 1970s muse. His man was dressed in a leisure suit and long hair. Grandma Izzy was a traditionalist. She used round chocolate candies for buttons and white icing for flourishes at the hands and feet. Clint went for an abstract design. He could have given Picasso a run for his money with the way he skewed the eyes. I would have never thought of putting a mouth at the neck, but it worked in a fun and disturbing way.

Maggie and Gretchen were hell-bent on winning. Maggie went for the fifties blue-jeans and leather-jacket look. If James Dean were a gingerbread man, he would have looked exactly like Maggie's cookie. Gretchen had more of a metrosexual thing going on. She bedazzled the shirt with a rainbow of nonpareils. Her gingerbread man sported short shorts and thigh-high boots. I didn't ask questions.

Mine was inspired by how I felt. I had warm fuzzies, and my heart filled with joy. I decided to create a sweater for my cookie. Its background was blue like Elias's eyes. Tiny hearts followed tiny rows of snowflakes until the entire sweater was complete. My cookie smiled knowing there was an entire evening of passion that lay ahead. Jeans and my best attempt at ski boots covered the lower half. The skis made from licorice would cement the win for me.

Elias kept his gingerbread man under wraps. At the big reveal, he presented his simple design. A big heart drawn in the center with red icing. A slice had been removed and in its place was my name. I'd taken a piece of his heart. There was no way I couldn't vote for that. A tear of happiness slipped from my eye.

When we were finished, Elias lined the treats up along the back of the bar and numbered them. We were all given a blank piece of paper and pen, then everyone wrote their choice on the tiny piece of paper and dropped it in the wine glass he sat on the counter.

There were seven votes to be had, and six went to Elias. One to me. Seeing his heart was open to love, his family voted unashamedly. Who could blame them? They loved him dearly. Was that what was happening for him though? I truly hoped so and was more than willing to look after his offered heart. He had already claimed mine.

He took a bow before he gave me a kiss. A hot passionate kiss in front of his entire family. At first, I was embarrassed, but then I got lost in his heat, and his family was forgotten.

CHAPTER 12

The night was full of celebration. The wine flowed freely, and so did Elias's kisses. I wasn't sure I would ever get enough of him. My heart said he was for real, but my mind kept telling me I was hired and he was the boss—a journey I had ventured down once before with horrible results. By his tenth or so kiss, I'd forgotten all about our scheme and had settled into the role of the beloved girlfriend.

We watched *A Christmas Carol* and when it was finished we played cards. I was awful at card games but could crush anyone in Monopoly. Next year we would have to get out the classic board game so I could bury them all. I had no mercy when it came to Monopoly. I bought property with abandon and traded with reserve. When it came to playing pieces, most people wanted the racecar. Not me, I was always the thimble. It was a sign of creativity, and it protected you from life's pokes.

Just after midnight, everyone hugged and exchanged Christmas greetings. Gretchen wanted to stay up and open presents. She was my age but managed to retain a child-like quality. We had begun to see her reasoning when she talked about sleeping in, but tradition won out in the end. So many Christmases had been missed, and there was no way to get them back. Besides, I was itching to get upstairs and begin where Elias and I had left off after dinner.

He had my ugly sweater off before I could close the door. "I've been craving you all night." He pressed against my body, pushing me toward the bed until my knees hit the mattress, and I fell back onto the soft comforter. It didn't take him long to remove my shoes, unbutton my jeans, and divest me of all clothing.

"Not fair." I lay naked in front of him, and he was fully clothed, again. "Why are you always dressed and I'm always naked?" I wanted him naked, too.

"Because I like you naked." He stood back and drank me in like an expensive wine. He slowly unbuttoned his shirt. It was like my own private striptease. If I'd had any singles, I would have been shoving them in his pants.

I leaned up on my elbows and watched him discard his shirt. I reflexively licked my lips as soon as he popped the snap on his jeans. The zipper popped tooth by tooth until it was completely undone and his jeans hung from his hips.

"You like?" he asked as he stuck his thumbs in the waistband of his pants.

"I like." I nodded my head and bit my lip. He was like a present that unwrapped itself.

When he pulled his pants and boxers off together, I was in awe. He was ready for me in all his fabulous glory. With muscles that reached from his ankles to heaven, it looked as though he had been chiseled from stone.

I sat up and began to explore him. Every inch. My tongue began to taste him. *Slowly.* I sank to my knees before him and worked my way up until I felt his knees weaken. The minute I took him in my mouth, his granite thighs seemed to crumble. I coaxed him to the bed where I laid him down and gazed at him like he had me. His body was perfection. Gutters ran between the sinewy muscles of his stomach, and when I pulled him deeper into my mouth, the hills and valleys became more pronounced.

He held his breath. I wanted to memorize every vein, every dip, and every curve of him, so I took my time. He panted and moaned and squirmed and reached. When it all seemed too much, he pulled me up his chest and crushed his mouth to mine. In between breaths, he told me the things I'd always wanted to hear.

"You're the most beautiful woman I've ever been with. Inside and out." He nipped at my neck and down to my breasts. "I haven't enjoyed a holiday like this in a decade, maybe a lifetime. Who would have thought, I'd hire a decorator and get a girlfriend in the bargain?"

"Girlfriend? Wasn't that a word we had promised not to use?" My hands explored the vast muscles of his chest and arms. These were the muscles that had carried the burden of disappointment for years. It was his turn to experience holiday bliss, and I would do my part to give it to him.

"It was banned when it wasn't true. What do you think you are to me, Cici? Like I said earlier, this is more than either of us could have imagined."

I spread my legs and straddled him, sinking onto his length. We both groaned. He filled me with more than his hardness. He filled me with desire. He filled me with hope for a future. He filled my mind with the notion we could have it all. Heavenly.

"What happens when I fall hopelessly in love with you?" I pressed my hands against his chest and raised and lowered myself in a slow rhythm. Every inch was give and take. I would give, and he would take. I would take, and he would give. Neither of us giving more than taking or vice versa. We were equals, sharing a moment to be remembered for all time.

"I will try to make that happen." He rolled us over, and this time he determined the pace. We made love in a languid fashion. He kissed me like it happens in the movies—that perfect kiss that melts your soul and ruins you for others. There would be no one else.

When he pulled out, his absence was felt immediately. I clawed at him, trying to go back to where we were seconds before, but he had other thoughts.

"It's my turn to worship your body."

I sucked in a gulp of air as his tongue slid down my neck, across my peaked nipples, and straight to the moisture between my thighs. Hot strokes made me thrash on the bed. I fisted handfuls of his comforter as my body pulsed beneath him. The build-up, exquisite. The time he kept me there, torture. Close to hyperventilating, he pulled my swollen flesh into his mouth and drew the most intense climax from my body. He didn't release me until every shudder had been sucked from my depths. He drew his tongue once more across me and climbed back up my body.

Settled between my legs, he entered me again, and our connection was complete. With every nerve ending on fire, I soared to new heights until he shuddered his release, and we landed safely together.

He collapsed next to me, drawing me close.

"Amazing." I was short on words but long on emotion. I could have wept at the connection I felt with him. I didn't think I'd ever truly made love to anyone until now. It required a leap of faith I'd never had with Ryan. The intimacy Elias and I shared scared me. What if he wasn't being completely honest with me about his feelings?

"Mmm."

"Am I the rebound girl?" It wasn't exactly what I'd planned to say. I wanted to say something like you're the best lover I've had. Hoping he would reciprocate, I didn't want to set him up.

He jolted, then turned to his side to look at me. "Cici, what I feel with you is more in every way than I felt with Becca. She has no place in our bed or our lives. We had a few dates. We slept together. I think we both tried to fill a void. There is no comparison to what she and I had and what you and I have."

I wanted to say I love you, but it was too soon. So I said, "I love that you feel that way." I kissed him gently and fell asleep tucked in the safety of his arms. I prayed I hadn't set my heart on a platter to be carved and served cold.

The morning sun broke through the window and lit up the room. I lay where I'd fallen asleep, in Elias's protective embrace. A glance at the clock on the nightstand showed it was early, only seven o'clock. Why I woke so early I couldn't imagine until I felt his erection press against my bottom.

I wiggled against him and listened to him groan. Was he up for round three? I was.

"I hope you slept well." His hands traveled my body, waking up my nerve endings one at a time. By the time he cupped the neatly trimmed juncture between my thighs I was tingling from want. I wanted him in the best possible way. Inside me. Immediately.

By his stone-hard presence, he needed no coaxing. He gave me what I wanted again and again until a kaleido-scope of colors shattered behind my closed eyes. Yesterday I was falling hard down a mountain, today I was falling hard for a man.

My body ached in the most delicious way. Every muscle throbbed, but I couldn't decide if it was due to the fall or the extracurricular activities we'd enjoyed over the last twenty-four hours. So much had happened in a day.

"I'll start the shower; you make the tea." With my arms stretched to the sky, I twisted and turned trying to unkink my muscles on the way to the shower.

"I'll be right back with your Earl Grey. Make that water hot. My body hurts."

"I cartwheeled down a mountain, and you're sore?" I looked over my shoulder and saw him watching me.

"I'll hurry." He tugged on his jeans and ran from the room. I don't think he could have moved faster even if I had lit his ass on fire.

The jets pulsed over my sore muscles. I poured his body wash into my hands and lathered myself from top to toe. After a lifetime of waiting, I shut off the water, dried off, and dressed. *No Earl Grey tea on the counter.* Maybe he'd gotten distracted by his family. It was probably Gretchen, and she had most likely torn into the presents.

Dressed in jeans and a pretty cashmere sweater, I trotted down the steps with more energy than I knew what to do with. My life was finally going in the right direction. There was hope for a happy ending in my personal and professional life. Yes, I had slept with the boss, but it had turned out well. More than well, I felt . . . content.

Standing at the bottom of the stairs was the entire Cole clan minus Elias. They all seemed to be staring at the front door. The hinges of their jaws hung open and a look of surprise was fixed on their faces.

When I followed their gazes, my heart was wrenched from my chest. Standing under the mistletoe was a beautiful blonde woman with her lips pressed to my man's lips.

CHAPTER 13

Elias pushed the woman away. "What are you doing here?"

Six of us stood together at the base of the stairs. The scene in front of us played out like a bad soap opera. "I changed my mind, Elias. You were counting on me, and I couldn't let you down. I came to meet your family and cook you dinner. We can work this out." The blonde's hand slid up the bare chest I had slept on. Her fingers brushed against the wisps of hair that had tickled my cheek only an hour ago. My stomach twisted as bile rose to choke me.

"Elias, who is that woman?" Izzy hadn't pulled any punches. Her question was direct and succinct. She wanted answers and, by her tone, she wanted them now.

The blonde stepped forward. "I'm Becca, Elias's girlfriend." If sound could be sucked from the air, it happened. The atmosphere crackled with questions, but not a soul moved or breathed.

Moments later, all heads turned to me. Accusations

were ripe in their eyes. I'd gained their trust through lies and deceit. I looked at Elias standing barefoot, dressed in jeans and nothing else. His eyes were filled with regret. Was it regret he'd been with me? I couldn't be certain. I'd caused too much pain to this family, and it was time to exit.

I pleaded silently for Elias to say something—anything that would cut through the tension. He stepped toward me, but Becca's hands halted him. Her fingers dug into the muscular arm I had lovingly caressed that morning. Taking two steps at a time, I ran upstairs to our room. *His room.*

I heard Elias tell Becca to go to the office. He called after me but there was nothing left to say. What we had was built on nothing but sexual chemistry and lies. I'd let myself get sucked into a fantasy. When would I learn? Why was my reality so . . . awful?

Whispers filtered up the stairs as I threw my clothes in a bag. When I heard the words *lie* and *sadness* and *hurt* I knew I had to leave right then. I couldn't bear to have Elias dismiss me and send me away. I would walk out with my head held high. I would maintain whatever dignity I could sink my nails into.

"Cici." Gretchen's voice startled me. "What's going on?"

I spun around to see her standing in the doorway. *Why hadn't I shut the door?*

I tossed my ugly sweater in my bag and started for the door. "Your brother will have to explain. I'm sorry." Whatever I left I could replace.

"You love my brother, don't you?" Her question seemed more like a declaration than a question. She needed to know the truth, but I was shamed by the truth. I'd fallen for my boss. I'd broken my rules and my heart.

"I do. I love your brother. It seems impossible given the time we've known each other, but life is funny that way. I'm sorry I deceived you all about who I was to Elias." I pushed past her and ran down the stairs.

She leaned over the rail and called out to me. "I've never seen my brother so in love, Cici. This will all get worked out. Don't give up." Her voice dimmed as I ran from the house to my car.

The engine roared to life. Elias appeared as the garage door opened, but I couldn't talk to him now. The tears were starting to fall, and I refused to let him see me so weak. I drove forward, leaving him standing barefoot in the snow calling after me.

How I made it down the mountain was a mystery. Thankfully the roads were empty. I drove down the center lane since I couldn't see through the tears obstructing my vision. When I pulled into my carport I sat and cried. Sobbed actually. I could barely breathe through my sobs. I had exposed my heart and, for a brief moment, thought I'd found someone who would protect it, but seeing his lips on Becca's while they stood under the mistletoe was more than I could handle. It was a repeat of my past.

Watching his family look at me like I had lied was unbearable. *They had seen my heart on my sleeve.* Even if there were something between Elias and me, it would never work out. I had destroyed his family's ability to trust me, and he could never love someone his family didn't trust. So important to him, he'd been willing to go to great lengths to please them. No. Whatever we shared was fleeting and now it was gone.

My house was empty. It looked like the Grinch had stolen Christmas. My little tree in the corner sagged from lack of water. A handful of ornaments lay on the bare floor next to it. The branches were all that was left now that the needles had fallen off. It was Christmas and the tree symbolized my life. Barren. Broken. Empty. *Merry Christmas to me.*

I made a cup of tea and curled up on the couch. It was time to reevaluate everything. I had run away from Los Angeles when things with Ryan had gone bad. He'd had too much influence on my career. Ryan Westland Design, the premier design company in Los Angeles, no one in their right mind left that firm. But I hadn't been in my right mind. I'd been in the mind of a cast-aside lover, and I'd needed to get as far away as possible.

This time I would stand my ground. Elias had some influence in his world of real estate, but he had no influence over my career. I had managed to succeed at nothing on my own since I'd arrived in Aspen. There was only one direction to travel when you'd hit rock bottom. Up.

Dance of the Sugar Plum Fairy broke the silence. *Mom.* What would I tell her?

"Hello." I smiled while I spoke. People said it changed your tone, and the last thing I wanted to do was cause my mom concern.

"Merry Christmas, honey. Do you love your slippers?" She gushed with excitement as she explained why she'd picked the penguin pattern. "You get it, right? Penguins and snow." My mom got excited over the simplest things.

"I love them, Mom. It's cold out right now so they will

come in handy." I had no idea what they looked like, but the fact she'd knitted them for me made me love them anyway. I'd have to figure out how to get them. All my gifts were still under the Cole Christmas tree. *It had been such a beautiful tree. Much like the fantasy.*

"We called last night, but you didn't answer." Her voice was muffled by the Christmas music blaring in the background. A Craig Christmas was full of movies, music, and mayhem. I could hear my brother, Cameron, belting out "Jingle Bells" in the background. *How I wished I were there right now.*

"I was over at a friend's. We played games and ate Chinese. It was a lot of fun. We even decorated gingerbread men." I thought about Elias's cookie and how he'd had a heart with a slice dedicated to me. My heart ached at the thought that just yesterday my life was so different.

"I wish you were here, sweetheart."

"I wish I were, too." It took every ounce of self-restraint to not cry.

"Take a picture of your slippers and send it to me. I want to make sure they fit right." Of course, she'd want a picture.

"I'll get right on that, Mom. I love you, and I'll talk to you soon." My father and brother yelled their greetings. When I hung up the phone, loneliness blanketed me. I turned off my phone and climbed into bed. I was determined to sleep through the day and avoid the remainder of Christmas this year.

Hours later I woke to a pounding on my door. Actually, it was more of a thumping. I dragged myself out of bed and trudged to the door. I really did need to talk to my landlord about a peephole. The only way to see who lay beyond the door was to open it, and I feared it might be Elias.

Gretchen. She stood on my doorstep with her arms full of presents. "May I come in?"

I felt relief and sadness all at once. Part of me wanted it to be Elias, but in my heart, I knew he wouldn't show. I'd seen Becca, and if you lined us up next to each other, there was no comparison. She was a diamond. I was a pearl or maybe the sand that caused the pearl.

I stood aside and let her enter. She walked in slowly, glancing around my home. It was so different from the luxury cabin she was staying in on Thunder Bowl. My home was a thousand square feet of *Design Challenge* meets *Secrets From a Stylist* with a dash of *Color Splash* thrown in for good measure.

"This place is so cool." She made her way into my curtain-lined living space. The air disturbance from our movement made the strips of fabric sway. "Don't tell me that's your tree?" She set the packages on my sofa and walked to the dead limb in the corner. Her hands reached for the fallen ornaments. Each one she tried to hang fell back to the floor. Some things just couldn't be fixed.

"What are you doing here?" I wrapped my arms around my waist and leaned against the wall.

"I came to spend Christmas with you." She began to stack the presents she brought on the table.

"No, it was so important to Elias that Christmas was perfect. You need to go home with your family."

"Well, here's the problem. I've always wanted a sister, and I finally had one with you. I'm not giving you up. If my brother was smart he would have been over here, not me." Her words sliced at my heart. Where was Elias? A vision of Becca's face rushed at me. He was with her.

She dug through the presents and handed me the one from my mother.

"It's slippers," I said. "You hardly know me, and what you do know is not the truth."

"Tell me the lies then." She sat back and stared at me.

"Um . . . I can't tell you the lies, but I can tell you the truth. Your brother hired me to stay through Christmas because his real girlfriend left him about a week ago. I met him on a job at his house. He had hired me to decorate because Becca had dropped the ball." My feet were feeling cold, so I slipped my finger under the paper and unwrapped my gift. Inside were the cutest penguin slippers ever. I brought them to my nose and smelled the scent of love. Tears pooled and threatened to fall.

"Okay, so where is the lie? You both said you had met on a job together." She shrugged in a *tell me something I don't know* way.

"I suppose, but it was a setup so you wouldn't know I wasn't the girlfriend." I crumbled the paper into a ball and tossed it toward the corner. The penguins fit perfectly. My mother knew me well.

"Hell, Cici, I think both of you forgot you weren't the girlfriend. I've never seen my brother look at any woman with as much love as he did you. He's in love with you." She sounded so confident, but if that were true, why wasn't he sitting in front of me?

"Gretchen, I was your brother's rebound girl. A quick fix until he could patch things up with Becca." The words spoken out loud filled me with regret. Regret it couldn't have been different. I leaned forward and rested my arms on my knees.

"He's not a rebound kind of man. He stayed single for years after Kimberly. If he were dating Becca it was purely for the sex." She cringed when she realized what she said. "It couldn't have been about the sex with you." The woman was digging a hole big enough to bury herself in. Flustered she said, "You know what I mean. My brother dedicated a cookie to you."

I smiled at the memory and then cried at the loss. "Last night was wonderful. This morning was wonderful until . . ." I was a snotty, crying mess, and Elias's sister didn't care. She pulled me into her chest and held me until I calmed down. "Is he home with your parents?" *With her?* I hiccuped with each breath I took.

"No, he took Becca to the airport. You should have waited. He gave her the boot immediately. Had my grandmother known she'd tossed him aside for a man with a brood of kids she would have put on her boots and kicked her skinny ass all the way to Denver."

"Denver? That's hours away. Oh . . . Christmas was ruined for all of you." My tears began again as soon as I realized everything Elias had tried to accomplish was gone.

"Becca used a car service, but they weren't available for the return trip. In order to keep Grandma Izzy out of jail, Elias put Becca in the car and took off." She pushed me away from her and rose. "I'm going to make us some tea."

I followed her into my kitchen. "How did you know where to find me?" It was odd she knew where I lived.

"I snooped in Elias's office. He had a check and an

addressed envelope made out to Chloe Craig of Craig Designs. That's what Cici is derived from, right?"

"Yes, but what about your family? What about dinner?" I pulled the tea bags from the cupboard while she filled the kettle with water.

"Oh, I'm pretty sure having you not cook dinner is a good thing. My mom knows how to kill a cow like no other. They won't starve to death."

With my head lowered I said, "I was happy to cook for you all. I bought books so I could follow the recipe."

"That's what I love about you, Cici. You don't even eat meat, and you planned to cook it for us anyway." She went about making the perfect cup of tea down to the honey. "I bet the thought of it made you want to retch."

"Well, the meat itself was okay, it's the fat I was having a hard time getting past. The damn recipe wanted me to trim the fat and set it aside for later." We both began to giggle. "I'm not sure I could have pulled it off, but I was willing to give it my best shot. In the end, we would have had plenty of side dishes. Those I could have mastered. They were things I make all the time. Sweet potatoes, mashed potatoes, and green bean casserole are right up my alley."

"I bet you make the best sides ever. Are you hungry? I am." She opened the freezer and groaned. There was one cheese pizza and a quart of chocolate chip ice cream.

"I don't have much to offer, but I can create a masterpiece with this pizza." I pulled it out, turned on the oven and went to work. "Does your family hate me?" It mattered to me. I liked them, and I didn't want them to loathe me.

"No, they hate Elias." Her answer was short and not so sweet.

"Why?" After I spread fresh garlic, sundried tomatoes, and artichoke hearts on the pizza, I tossed it in the hot oven.

"Because he thought we were so shallow. Him having a girlfriend didn't matter to any of us. Him being happy did. When you were there he was happy. Has he called you?"

"No. My phone hasn't rung all morning." Then it dawned on me I'd turned it off when I went to bed. I ran to the coffee table and powered it up. Eleven missed messages. Two from my mom and nine from Elias.

His last one was only minutes ago. Just as my finger pressed play, someone knocked on the door. My heart bounced in my chest as I rushed toward it. When I opened it, Grandma Izzy and Uncle Fritz were on my doorstep. I stood aside and let them in.

"I'm not happy about your little ruse, my girl, but I'm certain you're the one for my grandson." She plopped a bowl of salad in my hands and walked in. Uncle Fritz nodded and carried what looked like sweet potato casserole. I went to shut the door, but a foot shoved inside stopped my progress.

"Merry Christmas, Cici." Maggie walked in with what looked like a bowl of green beans and a bowl of quinoa. Behind her was Clint with several bottles of wine and a platter of rolls. "Set the table, we're hungry."

They all went to work in my kitchen like they owned the place. I set the table then stood back and watched in awe as this family came together. The only one missing was Elias. When a knock sounded at the door I knew it was him. It wasn't a pounding demand for entry but a tentative knock.

All activity stopped. Every eye watched as I walked to the door. When I cracked it open, Elias stood with a tree in his hand and a question in his expression. He looked past me to his family. I could see the apology as if it had come from his mouth. He was sad, and I was a sucker for sad.

I stepped aside and let him in. Where he found a tree on Christmas day I couldn't guess, but I hoped he didn't pay a fortune for it. It wasn't in much better shape than the one I had. He handed the tree to his father and pulled me into his arms.

"I'm so sorry, Cici. She wasn't supposed to come. Becca and I were over, and you and I were on our way to falling in love. No . . . that's not right."

I breathed in the scent of orange and cloves. "It's not?" I wrapped my arms around his waist and held on.

"No. We had way more than forty hours under our belt. We are in love. I'm in love with you, Cici. Please . . . I want that back."

My heart swelled in my chest. He loved me, and I still loved him.

"I didn't stop loving you, Elias. I just stopped hoping you would feel the same."

"Would you guys kiss and make up? An old woman could die of starvation before you two lock lips." Elias was right. His grandmother was ornery enough to outlive us all.

We needed no further coaxing. His mouth crushed into mine, his kiss hot and demanding. If I didn't live in an open-floor concept, I would have taken him behind the curtains and had my way with him. Instead, I whispered in his ear. "You owe me tea."

"I love you, and I'll give you everything. Tea included."

"Oh shush, you two, let's eat, then we can get on with the presents and the important stuff." Izzy was getting testy.

"And what would the important stuff be, Mother?" Maggie looked at her mother, her head tilted in question.

"We've got to clear out of here so these kids can start working on my great grandbabies."

CHAPTER 14

Full of vegetarian delights including a cheese pizza, we sat around the newly decorated tree and opened presents. Elias had filled his trunk before he'd arrived. His family was hell-bent on having me for the holidays, and when he'd said he was coming to my house, they'd given him a list of things to do and then driven quickly to beat him here. I'm not sure what their intent was, but somehow I felt they were protecting him. Or maybe they were taking the time to welcome me on their own terms.

Everyone loved their gifts, especially Clint who teared up when his son gave him the gift of time. They would be fishing in the spring. Elias was touched I'd purchased some special fishing gifts for him as well.

Gretchen loved her Limoges box and gold pine cones necklace. Maggie was over the moon with her cashmere scarf. I laughed my head off when Izzy opened her package and found a year's subscription to Live Alert. Elias was simply looking after his granny. And since

Uncle Fritz spent a great deal of time with his mother, Elias bought him noise-canceling headphones.

I was gifted with more lavender products than a person could use in a lifetime, a brand new Kindle with a gift card and a year's worth of hardback books straight from the 100 must-read list. His gifts were generous and heartfelt. He'd listened to me and heard me.

The Coles bought me the softest ski gloves and hat. They also hired the same ski instructor to do what he does best—watch me tumble down the hill.

In spite of the drama, Christmas had turned out to be wonderful with the warmth and happiness of any Norman Rockwell scene. My little home had never been so full of love. When we had finished the bottles of wine Clint had lifted from Elias's collection, the Coles packed up their presents and left. They kissed us both goodbye and told us they would see us tomorrow.

When the door shut, Elias pulled me straight to the bed. With the finesse of a magician, he had me naked and on display for him.

"Mr. Cole, we have talked about this before. You are fully clothed, but I'm naked as the day I was born. This won't do."

"You're right." He pulled a small wrapped package from his back pocket and set it on my bare stomach. I stared at it for a minute before I pulled the paper off and opened the box to find a Limoges Christmas tree. When I popped it open a necklace with the letter C fell out.

"Are you afraid I can't spell my name?"

"As a matter of fact, I am. I'm sure you realize Chloe and Cici begin with a C, but I want you to think about how things will end, and Cole has a nice ring to it, don't you think? Someday, Chloe Craig, I'm going to make you want to be Chloe Cole, and this will be a daily reminder of that goal."

He placed the necklace around my neck. The C hung above my heart. He kissed me there first and let his lips travel across every dip and curve of my body. His love was the healing balm to my fractured heart. *Could this divine man really be mine?*

"Are you going to undress?" I asked breathlessly.

"Are you in a hurry? We have a lifetime."

"The day is fading, Elias, and you owe me a lot of Cole for Christmas." And that's exactly what I got. Again and again. Merry. Christmas. To. Me.

It wasn't a wise move to sleep with the boss, so when we woke up, I asked him to fire me. I'd rather be broke than loveless. I could always find a job, but there was only one Elias Cole, and he'd given himself and his family to me for Christmas.

Back at his house the next day, we sat in front of the big Christmas tree with his family. "Hey babe, you won the gingerbread contest, so where is Christmas next year?" All eyes were on Elias.

"I'm thinking we should converge on the Craig's next year. Didn't you say you had a brother Gretchen's age?"

The End.

GET A FREE BOOK.

Go to www.authorkellycollins.com

ABOUT THE AUTHOR

International bestselling author of more than thirty
novels, Kelly Collins writes with the intention of keeping
the love alive. Always a romantic, she blends real-life
events with her vivid imagination to create characters and
stories that lovers of contemporary romance, new adult,
and romantic suspense will return to again and again.

For More Information
www.authorkellycollins.com
kelly@authorkellycollins.com

www.ingramcontent.com/pod-product-compliance
Lightning Source LLC
Chambersburg PA
CBHW070509200726

48293CB00007B/2464